CW00745733

Deleted

Also by Sylvia Hehir
Sea Change

Praise for *Sea Change*:

"I genuinely found it hard to put this book down to get on with my day." Shona MacLean – author of the Alexander Seaton series.

"This is a haunting portrayal of a young lad, coping on his own in the best way he can, whilst many of the adults around him let him down … This story is about friendships, bad decisions, mistakes and the complexity of life." Liz Mistry – crime novelist.

"An excellent novel, engaging, gripping, powerfully written and emotionally compelling for teenage readers." Armadillo Magazine

"A dark coming-of-age story, a mystery and a tale of friendship & betrayal all rolled into one." Stuart McLean – Goodreads reviewer.

"I was gripped from the beginning by this easy-to-read and engaging thriller and I really appreciated Sylvia Hehir's portrayal of the setting… with characters who were well drawn, relatable and believable…" Bridget E. – NetGalley reviewer.

"Although it starts with the discovery of a body, arguably it is the teenage themes – of identity; responsibility; friendship – that take centre stage. The sensitive portrayal of the demands on a teen carer is welcome and laudable." Maggie McShane – online reviewer.

"Sea Change by Sylvia Hehir was a pleasant surprise … Love comes into it, and there are many secrets and much mistrust. And when you are 16 or 17 you don't share with 'responsible' adults, and what happens happens. This book is a real page turner, and I'm glad I read it." Bookwitch – blogger.

Deleted

Sylvia Hehir

Garmoran Publishing

First Published in Great Britain 2020
Copyright © Sylvia Hehir 2020

All rights reserved. No part of this publication may be reproduced, in any form or by any electronic or mechanical means, including information storage and retrieval systems, without the prior permission in writing from thepublisher.

ISBN: 978-1-913510-03-9

All characters and events in this publication, other than those clearly in the public domain, are fictitious and any resemblance to real persons, living or dead, is purely coincidental and not intended by the author.

The moral right of the author has been asserted.

Cover art © Hilary James

A CIP catalogue record for this book is available from the British Library

Printed and bound in United Kingdom by Biddles, Kings's Lynn

Published by
Garmoran Publishing
Ardnamurchan, Scotland

www.garmoranpublishing.com

I laughed when I saw the bin sign appear on my new mobile as I deleted Amy's name.

I would have stuffed Amy in a bin for real after all she'd done.

One

'Aaaahh. At last,' I screamed on Christmas Morning, flinging bits of wrapping paper around the living room.

Mum came thumping downstairs in her jammies to see what was the matter.

'It's half six, Dee,' she said, quite grumpily to be honest, considering it was the season to be jolly.

'Yes! You beauty,' I said, throwing Mum the fancy Christmassy box my present from Dad had arrived in. She caught it skilfully before stamping in to the kitchen.

My hints to Dad – who was currently having his turkey dinner on a sun-soaked beach somewhere – had worked. He's a transport consultant and works all over the world. Good thing: he sends home lots of packages containing wacky presents. Bad thing: he's rarely home. So this year there were no surprise presents under the tree. No disturbing shadow puppets from Bali or nose flutes from Bolivia; just a normal, top-spec mobile phone.

I couldn't wait to try out it out but Mum had her own plans, and me sitting playing with a mobile didn't enter in to them. I'm sure baby Jesus doesn't insist on

3

slavery and incarceration as part of the celebrations for his birth. I said to Mum – while she was still listening to me that was – we can just have beans on toast if we want. No one will know. But she carried on with the whole works, then expected me to help clear up. At least it gave us something to do.

Completely immobilised by Christmas dinner, I was finally allowed to retire to my room. Snuggled under my downie, and with Ted maintaining an appreciative silence as I showed him the features on my phone, I began downloading my contacts. No way was I keeping Amy's number. It hadn't taken me long to work out it'd been her who'd fed the twisted half-truths to John – my first and only proper boyfriend let me add – until he didn't know who or what to believe.

So, as I reached Amy's name, I hit the delete button. And with a rush of blood that made my head spin and left my ears tingling, I suddenly imagined her wedged in a big, black bin, her legs waving about.

It was no more than she deserved, and yes, I laughed out loud.

Two

'Get your feet off the coffee table,' Mum said next day as I was trying – not at all successfully, obviously – to pretend I was taking a nap while I played a game on my phone.

'Sorry for existing,' I said before hurrying off to my bedroom.

Who in their right mind had invented Boxing Day anyway? Christmas had already lasted FOREVER. To be fair to Mum, she had tried hard but there is only so much fun two people can have with an impossible jigsaw and a Scrabble board when you can't use KNOB.

It was the same for the rest of the gang. We'd all had to suffer family Christmases. I couldn't wait for life to get back to normal. It had been two whole days!

I was even annoying Ted. He might be my faithful, old teddy bear but I have learnt that there are limits to his tolerance. In an attempt to put my life in to some sort of order by shifting all the furniture around in my bedroom, I was trying to find new places for him to sit. He finally came back on my bed after experiencing life on top of my wardrobe, next to my speaker and, least comfortable of all he assured me, squashed between my desk and the wall. Ted is sixteen too, younger than me by one day and, lucky thing, he's never seen life outside of the house. He's never had a so-called mate dish dirt on him.

'We are so over John, aren't we?' I said as I put my head on Ted's soft belly. I had to agree with him that after five weeks and three days, I really ought to be. 'And Tom Higgins did seem interested in me the other night. I don't think he noticed my wobbly hips.'

Ted kept quiet on that one. He's sensible like that.

Fortunately, just as I was fearing for my sanity, Frankie escaped from her family and – as a best friend should – arrived to save me. She floated in to my bedroom, her silky cheeks made rosy by the chilly winds. Even the winter weather seemed intent on improving her already good looks.

'Let's get you out of the dumps then,' she said.

She threw a pile of bags on the floor – a satisfying clink of glass coming from one of them – turned up Fat Boy Slim and pulled me off the bed. We were soon prancing around, checking out each other's zany Christmas gifts.

'Fetching,' Frankie said as I tried on the frilly, pink nightie her granny had sent.

'Enticing,' she added as I accessorised it with my new black ankle boots and did high kicks in time to the beats. We crashed to the floor in a final dance frenzy as the track finished, panting to get our breath back.

James Bond action music filtered up from below. Mum was taking timeout from the never-ending washing up and was watching her movie.

Frankie recovered first. She gathered up scattered clothing then snuggled on the bed to better admire my mobile.

'You've got Tom Higgins on then?'

'You don't think I should?' I said, my stomach tying itself in knots.

'Well ... We don't know much about him.'

'You have to admit he is gorgeous though. Those moody looks.' I climbed on the bed beside her. 'And you're sure you're not interested?'

'Definitely not! Although yes, I agree,' she gazed up at the ceiling, 'he is a hunk...'

'I can hear a but.'

'Well ... he's so big.'

'I don't think he's any taller than John.'

'Maybe not. He just seems to take up too much space. And those clothes. A woolly jumper for goodness sake. He doesn't fit in. I mean, who would he hang around with?' She fixed me with her hazel eyes. 'You know I'm right.'

'But those dimples when his face breaks in to that slow, sexy smile.'

'Just because a boy pays attention to you doesn't mean you have to fall in love with him.'

Frankie, as usual, was trying to make me see things her way. Tom Higgins had only been in the village for about a week.

'You're barely over your breakup with John,' she added.

As if there was any chance of me forgetting. I wasn't going to start discussing that again. My nerves wouldn't stand it. I was still bewildered by what had taken place that day. Somehow, the love of my life right up until that very moment was skulking in my bedroom doorway with a wretched look on his face and I was shouting: 'If I never see you again it will be too soon.'

I hadn't seen him since.

I rearranged Frankie's fringe that she'd swept out of her eyes and spoke in my softest and wisest way. 'Yes, I know. Thank you. I love you very much.'

She fiddled with her earrings – a sure sign she was working up to a big lecture – but my mobile chirped in with its delivery tone. Frankie scowled and tossed it to me. It was a message from Tom Higgins: 'I'll be in le club for a while. Maybe see you there? Tom'

I read it, then poked her. 'Come on, we're off to Le Club and we'll have to walk. Mum can't be disturbed when she's watching a movie. I can't wait to learn to drive.'

'But we're almost bananas in pyjamas,' was her pathetic reply.

'We can take Tom to Sandi's party.'

'Like that's going to make it better,' she muttered, sounding pretty peeved. 'And you said you didn't want to go to the party,' she went on. 'Said you didn't want to see Amy dolled up like a Christmas tree flashing her bazoomas at everyone, even though I'd told Sandi we'd probably be going.'

'Ah, but that was before Tom Higgins messaged me,'

8

I said. I was enjoying our girlie night in but the well-timed message had shaken me back to my senses.

'And I was about to try out your new eyelash curlers,' was her next stab at emotional blackmail. This time I was saved by Harry Styles. I keep telling Frankie that a Harry ring tone is not a for a hot chick but does she listen to me? Well yes, she has to but she rarely takes any notice of me. By the time she'd got her ancient battered phone out of her bag, the caller had given up. There was a message though. It was from Rhona, who always has all the goss.

'Hey, have you heard about Amy?' I read as Frankie leaned over and showed me.

'I wonder what's happened?' she said, more to herself than me.

I laughed at the sweet turn of fate. 'Well, there's only one place to go to find out. We'd better get to Le Club,' I said. 'Shall I wear my strawberry strappy dress or jeans? Are stockings in or skanky at the moment?'

'In.'

She picked up her new Christmas t-shirt and her old, scruffy, well-loved Levi's and accepted defeat gracefully. I pocketed my mobile with a gloating smile lurking around my too-big-for-my-liking lips.

Snowflakes drifted around in the wind and we tried running some of the way to keep warm as we set off through the village but my heels were too high to manage more than a few paces before I stumbled. Some younger kids huddled in the bus shelter, a couple of them smoking furtively. We passed by our old primary school with the cut-out paper snowflakes stuck to the windows; then further along, out of reach of the village streetlights, the granite-built police station, intimidating in the darkness.

Le Club was heaving. All the folk in the village who like to get out and party were there. A row of silver haired sherry-sippers lined the bay window. Their main occupation was making sideways comments about the gang of middle-aged women mum-dancing to the music that blared out from the speakers above the bar. Lads who work up in town but who'd come home for Christmas, propped up the bar and argued with the oldies. Actually, some of the lads are quite smart and can be fun to flirt with but none could compare to Tom Higgins.

And there he was, standing at the bar, his brown leather jacket slung over his broad shoulders. Frankie did her usual trick and darted in to Le Ladies. Her eyelashes being cruelly neglected, she needed to apply another twenty coats of mascara before being seen in public. Rhona was sitting in the poolroom so there was no chance of nonchalantly passing Tom. I dashed in to the Ladies myself.

I'd no sooner closed the door than Rhona pushed it open again, forcing me and Frankie to squash up against the sink.

'Look at this,' she said, pushing her glasses up her nose and fishing her mobile out of her voluminous bag. She brought up a photo on the display that took a bit of working out.

Eventually, I made out the black plastic sides of a rubbish bin and a pair of shoes sticking out the top. And they weren't just any shoes. They were Amy's spanking-new, hot-pink suede shoes, still attached to Amy's 15 denier stockinged legs. Although there were several holes in the stockings. A prickly heat flushed up my neck and cheeks, and my fingers trembled as I passed the mobile to Frankie.

'Poor Amy, what happened?' squealed Frankie.

'She was going over to Jason's when she was chased by a huge dog. It cornered her outside the Spar. She tried to climb over the fence and fell into the rubbish bin.' Then Rhona whispered, 'We don't know whose dog it is. Amy thinks it might belong to that Tom Higgins. It'd disappeared by the time her mum came.'

'She didn't remember the keeping safe from dangerous dogs rap then?' Frankie said. It was a wee song we'd learnt in primary school about standing still and tucking our hands in our pockets when in the presence of dangerous beasts. It went to a funky rap rhythm to help us remember it but fear had obviously driven it out of Amy's memory.

'Not that her skinny rib dress would protect her much,' Rhona mused.

'Poor Amy,' Frankie said. 'Did you get her out all right?'

'Amy's mum came to help. I phoned Jason first but he didn't seem that bothered. And I wasn't going any closer on my own if that monster was still hanging around,' Rhona said. 'I took a photo to prove it to Jason. Some use he is as a boyfriend. I don't know why Amy sticks with him. He said she was making a big fuss about nothing.'

I wanted to point out that Amy would have made sure Jason knew all about her incident without any photographic evidence but I was completely dumbstruck. My pulse was racing. My brain ached. The picture on Rhona's phone was exactly what I'd imagined when I'd deleted Amy's name from my contact list.

I leaned against the wall while Frankie continued to get the lowdown on the whole sorry episode. 'Where is she now?' she asked.

'At home.'

'Amy's not going to the party then?' I managed to ask. My voice was shaky and Frankie gave me a questioning look.

'Oh yeah, she is. Her mum's taking her up. I thought you'd be there already,' Rhona said to me.

'Why?'

'Cos John's there.'

'John's at his aunt's in Edinburgh,' I said, fairly confidently. He'd taken me at my word and hadn't made contact since our breakup. I do have my spies though.

'Well that's where you're wrong. He went with his mum to his Aunt Sabina's for Christmas and they've driven up today,' Rhona said.

I turned to peer in the dimly lit mirror. I wasn't going to let Rhona see her information about John affected me in any way.

'Oh, Dee,' Frankie whispered, 'I don't think it would be a good idea to turn up at the party with Tom if John is there.'

'You've got your eyes on Tom Higgins, have you?'

Rhona said, delighted to discover another bit of juicy news. 'You'd better get out there quick then,' she said. 'Jimmy Johnson is boring him to tears. He might even be grateful enough to buy you a drink; you look like you need one. Watch out for his dog though.'

Luckily for Rhona, my mobile chimed in again.

'Heading to party. Want to come? Tom'

I messaged back before my better judgement got a look in. 'Be with you in a mo. Dxx'

'Well, Rhona, much as we would like to stay here in the ladies' loo talking to you all night, Frankie and I have a party to go to,' I said, steadying my hand and applying more lippy.

'I'm going now myself,' Rhona said. 'And I hope you know what you're letting yourself in for with that Tom Higgins. We know precious little about him except...'

'Yeah, yeah, 'cept he works on the hydro scheme and his dad used to come here collecting whelks,' I finished for her.

Ten minutes later we were all squashed in one of the cars heading for the party. Frankie, Rhona and Tom filled the back seat and I was sprawled across the three of them, my bottom safely nestled in Tom's lap and my peep toe stilettos poking Rhona in the crotch.

Three

The party was in full swing. Outside the house a bare-chested lad, wearing only a kilt and hiking boots, was dancing with the fat, plastic Santa that stood in the garden. Santa's reindeer companion lay knocked on his side, his red nose beaming intermittently.

Loud bass beats from indoors accompanied the flashing icicles on the roof.

Was John in there? And, more to the point, was I ready to see him again?

Tom followed close behind me. Frankie took hold of my hand and led me in through the gate.

'Come in,' Sandi called, leaning out of a window. Her mum and dad had believed her when she'd said she'd rather stay home and revise than go with them to Tenerife. Fat chance of my mum ever going away and leaving me.

A heady mix of incense sticks and fresh sweat hit us full in the face as we piled in to the tiny hallway. Bunches of mistletoe hung wilting above our heads. A hand grabbed my arm and I was pulled backwards in to a steamy armpit. I fought my way to a corner of the living room where Sandi had put out bowls of crisps and a jug of punch on a small table.

Her family had really gone for it with the decorations indoors too. Paper chains, strands of shiny tinsel, strings of Christmas cards and bunches of brightly coloured balloons filled every bit of wall space. I felt dizzy and hemmed in.

I'd lost Tom and Frankie in the crowds but Rhona was standing beside the window. I poured out two large glasses of punch and sidled towards her. The fruity, spiced wine trickled down my throat and my cheeks flushed. I was tempted to join the hordes jumping up and down to early Primal Scream – Frankie must have got to the playlist – but I didn't recognise many people and Rhona said she didn't want to dance.

'I want to sit down,' she said when she'd downed her drink but all the seats were filled with couples so closely clamped together it looked like an alien species with writhing, intertwining limbs had landed and taken over the soft furnishings.

A girl was blowing bubbles across the swelling tide of bodies, those nearby her jumping up to waft them around. Then I spotted Tom across the living room, standing beside the hi-fi. He pushed up the sleeves of his thick knit jumper and scrolled through the playlist. A shudder rippled through the pit of my belly as he combed his fingers through his straggly black hair. I started to push people aside to get to him but then – horrors – I came across Amy and John snuggled in the corner of a comfy sofa.

Good old John. Safe old John – sitting beside that double-crossing Amy. He was cradling her head and she was trying to hide a self-satisfied grin.

When John spotted me, he quickly stood up and a frown crossed his face. We made a few awkward stammers to each other.

Then he said, 'Amy thinks that ... that you might know something about her accident.'

'What do you mean?' I felt a blush spread right down to my neck. 'I don't know anything. I wasn't anywhere ... What makes you think—?'

Amy narrowed her eyes. 'Come off it, Dee,' she said. 'Rhona, like, just told me you looked really guilty when she showed you that photo of me. And I've never seen that dog around before. I bet it belongs to Tom Higgins, and you, like, came with him tonight.'

John just stood there, nodding like a pompous nodding thing.

I looked into his eyes. 'Rhona never said anything of the kind. You can't be suggesting ... You think because—'

'I don't know what to think anymore, Dee,' John said, sounding about ninety.

Amy was obviously lying again. My legs sagged. How could John believe that I'd known anything about it? He was even going along with Amy that I was involved somehow.

Then, like a slap across the face, the idea hit me that they might be right. Perhaps it had been sloshing around my brain up until then. But there was no budging the thought once it jumped in front of my eyes.

Was I the cause of Amy's mishap?

There was no rational explanation. I certainly hadn't plotted to set some crazy mutt on Amy and scare her off. But I had imagined that very same picture when I'd deleted Amy's name from my new phone.

My mind was in a whirl. I couldn't face any more from John and Amy. I scanned the room. There was still no sign of Frankie, and Tom had disappeared again too. I swallowed hard and set my face straight. Keeping my head held high, I elbowed through the crowds and went into the kitchen.

It was surprisingly empty but Frankie was in there mixing drinks. 'Here you go chick,' she said handing me a fizzing plastic glass. 'You look like you need a good time. And stop biting your lip.' The drink was sharp on my tongue and cold in my head.

I started to tell Frankie my fears about my phone.

'You mean the phone somehow predicted what happened to Amy?'

'Well sort of. I don't know.' I lowered my voice. 'Do you think I caused it?'

'What on earth makes you think that? How could you have?'

I spoke quickly to try to get rid of the idea. 'But it was exactly like I imagined. How could that happen?'

'A coincidence. Either that or you're going psychic on me. And steady on with that.' I'd drunk down most of the contents of the glass.

'So, you don't think I made it happen?'

Frankie gave me her exasperated look. I stopped

talking when Rhona came in supporting a swaying Sandi. Rhona propped her up beside me while she fetched a glass of water.

'Who's this fresh meat ye've brought with ya, Dee?' Sandi slurred in my ear. I was nearly knocked out by the fumes coming off her.

'Tom Higgins you mean? Bit fit, isn't he?' I said.

'Where's 'e from?'

'He's from Sunderland,' Rhona chipped in.

I nodded along with her, not wanting to appear a complete dope brain.

'He's on work placement at the hydro scheme,' Rhona added in her know-it-all way. 'Dee's hoping to show him a few of the sights.'

'Doesn't matter where 'e's from when 'e looks that good. Hadn't you better get back before someone else takes a bite of the cherry?' she said, making rude gestures in my face.

It was true. I hadn't spoken to Tom since we'd arrived. The party was fast becoming a nightmare. I needed something good to happen. I downed my drink and left the kitchen.

Tom was on the stairs. He wrapped a warm hand around mine as I tottered towards him and we climbed the stairs hand in hand.

When we reached the landing, he clamped his mouth over my lips and held me tightly around my waist with one arm.

He was interested then.

He moved an exploring hand over my back and

down my hips.

A few people jostled past us, joining the queue for the bathroom. Then I felt his fingers find the top of my stocking. I stiffened. I wasn't ready for this. We'd barely spoken a dozen words to each other all night.

He manoeuvred me around and we stumbled across the landing.

He was muttering something in my ear, something about a drink but I couldn't tell what he was saying. My brain had switched off listening. All I could focus on was what Tom's hands were doing. I staggered backwards through an open door in to Sandi's old playroom. A muffled quietness clicked on as he closed the door behind us. The rhythmic thud and chorus chant now belonged to a party far away.

A blind half covered the one small window in the room, partially blocking the orange glow that crept in from a distant street lamp. We lurched across the wooden floor as he guided me further in to the room. I stumbled against a pile of cardboard boxes and I grabbed a My Little Pony lampshade sticking out at an awkward angle from a shelf. He quite gently pulled me back towards him but again he clamped his lips on to mine. His arms held me tighter.

I pulled away from him. 'Don't. I'm not...'

He flickered some sort of reply. 'You came with me—'

'No. No,' I managed to splutter. A wave of nausea swept over me and I turned my head to gasp for air. I pushed against his chest. 'No.' I banged my fists against him and he dropped his arms against his side.

Tom sprang away from me like a startled cat and dashed out of the bedroom door.

Four

Hot tears rushed down my foolish face. Burning bile hit the back of my throat. I squatted in the middle of the room, listening to my heartbeat.

The sounds of drunken singers came up from outside and I peered through the window. A Conga line snaked out of the front door, past the still jolly Santa and around the garden. Then Tom rushed past the crowd and through the garden gate. He gave a quick glance back at the house, pulled up his jacket collar and hurried away.

I checked my clothing. One strap of my slinky dress was broken but apart from that everything seemed pretty much okay. I waited for my racing pulse to slow down.

How had things gone so badly wrong? I fancied Tom. Not just because of his looks either. He'd seemed shy and interesting. I'd wanted to talk to him, get to know him better. Was I mistaken about him?

But he had stopped when I called out.

I got up and left the playroom. Frankie was bouncing up the stairs.

'There you are. Guess what's happened,' she said.

I shook my head, not sure that I could trust my voice.

'Jason came in and saw Amy with John. They all had a big quarrel and Jason finished with ... What's happened?' she said, scanning my face. She put her firm hands under my elbows and pulled my trembling body towards her. She glanced behind me into the playroom. 'Where's Tom? What's he done?'

I slumped against her. 'Nothing. He did nothing.'

'Tell me.' She lightly brushed a tear from my cheek.

'Nothing. Really. Leave it. Just leave it.'

'If that wee shite...' she said looking down the stairs.

'He's done nothing. It's probably me being—'

'Don't even think you've done anything ... Where is he anyway?'

'Don't make a fuss, Frankie. I've had enough. I just want to go home.'

She ran a hand over my hair. 'Okay. I'll give Dad a ring,' she said calmly, steering me downstairs.

So, with Frankie leading me by one hand and my shoes hanging from the other, we made our way to the back door to wait.

I'd barely got through my bedroom door when the message tone sounded on my mobile. Without even checking it, I slid it across the floor and flopped on my bed.

I closed my eyes: my head thumped. I opened them again: the posters on my walls swam up and down.

I slipped off my stockings, crawled under my downie and clasped the hottie mum had put in for me.

But sleep wouldn't come. I couldn't stop my mind churning over the events of the evening. I should have listened to Frankie. I'd gone off with a boy I hardly knew, a boy everyone was warning me about.

I fished around for Ted. He squashed in beside me, his fur tickling my nose.

'And now Amy is free from Jason,' I told Ted. 'She'll get her claws in John. You wait and see.'

Why on earth was I still bothered about John when he was prepared to believe anyone's stories about me? He'd even seemed ready to believe I'd been involved in Amy's accident.

Just like he'd believed Amy when she told him that I'd cheated on him.

For about the thousandth time, I played over our breakup again. I'd gone ballistic when he'd stood there calmly in my bedroom and asked if what he'd heard was true.

Hadn't I told him often enough how I felt about him I'd said. 'And you still don't trust me?' I'd screeched.

He apologised straight off and said of course he believed me; he was wrong to suspect me. Holding out his arms he asked would I not forgive him. But the pain caused by his doubt was like a punch in my guts.

I wanted him to feel pain too. I picked up anything close to hand and threw it all at him: books, bottles of perfume, magazines. He stood stock still, accepting my rage. But his face fell in shock when I took off the gold heart locket and chain that he'd lovingly fastened around my neck on my birthday and threw that too. He let it dangle from his fingers for a few moments before scrunching it up in his fist.

Who the hell was calling me in the middle of the night? My phone was ringing from underneath my set of drawers. I stumbled out of bed, tripped on a shoe and cracked my elbow on my desk.

The display told me it was Tom. No way was I answering his call. I wanted nothing to do with him. I scrolled down my contacts, hit the delete button when I got to his name, and switched off.

Next thing I knew mum had placed a mug of tea on my bedside cabinet and was pulling the downie from off my head. She pursed her lips like she was going to whistle. A row was coming.

'Yes, it is Christmas,' she said, 'and having a drink is one thing but coming home in that state is another. I thought you had more sense.'

And with that she left me with a banging headache. Squinting in my mirror I saw that my eyes, normally my best feature I like to think, looked like I'd had poached egg implants.

It was midmorning but the world outside the window was half dark. Hailstones clattered noisily against the glass.

I retrieved my phone, switched it on, and opened a message from Frankie. 'Call me when you wake up. We're going to a gig. Pick you up half five.'

Five

By five o'clock mum had given me a spot of lunch and I was sitting gazing out the front window watching for Frankie. My eyes were still a bit blotchy but I'd made an effort to tackle the evening, slapping on the concealer. I'd decided to wear my crimson skirt with a white t-shirt. I was surprised to see John's van, with its 'Sound John' lettering on the side, pull up outside. For some reason, I'd expected Frankie's dad to be taking us. Frankie jumped out of the passenger seat, and with her tippy toe run, she sprinted up to our front door. We had a heated discussion as I let her in.

'I can't go in that van.'

'Why not?' She shrugged. 'There's plenty of room for three.'

'You know what I mean. I told you what John said last night.'

'You don't need to take any notice of that. He was worried about Amy.'

She wrapped a scarf around my neck and guided me out.

There was an icy silence in the van as we scuttled along the single-track lanes. I took my usual place in the middle seat with my knees close to John's denim clad legs. The wipers dragged freezing rain across the windscreen. Frankie plugged herself in to her music and the strangled sounds of Christmas songs added to the gloom.

John fiddled with the heater switch trying to bring a bit of warmth to the van. I stole a look at his sinewy muscles exposed by his rolled-up sleeves as he expertly took the bends and changed gears.

I'd first fallen for him when I saw him leap onto the stage to set up a band for the school talent show. He was two years above me and I thought he wouldn't even give me a second look. He'd never paid much attention to girls; he was intent on following his own passions, his own dreams. Then I'd got involved with helping the school band and when they competed at a Battle of the Bands gig, I'd worked alongside John. We easily slipped into a friendship, and then more.

Oh! Why had he believed Amy? Why hadn't he kept faith in me?

He gave a quick glance in my direction.

'Not really dressed for helping out, are you?'

'Thought you might have found yourself another skivvy,' I said.

'What do you mean?'

'No, of course, Amy can't be expected to get her hands dirty carting about amps and speakers and cables, can she?'

'I am not seeing Amy,' he said through clenched teeth.

'No? Well, now Jason's out of the equation you can correct that can't you.'

A police car came flying towards us and John pulled over in to a passing place.

After a few tense moments he said, 'I thought you might be busy with someone else tonight.' And when I didn't respond he continued. 'I heard you were quite friendly with Tom Higgins last night.'

'You seem to hear a lot, John.' Then I forced myself to say, 'There's no harm in me being friendly is there?'

'No. No harm I suppose.'

John swung the van in to the village hall car park and backed up to the doorway. There was a single light showing in the hall and Frankie ran in. Seconds later she came back with the janitor and joined John at the back of the van. I ditched my pride and jumped out of the van too. I pulled John's duffle coat from behind his seat and buttoned it up over my otherwise impractical clothes. John smiled at me and threw me my trainers which were still in the back of the van. I changed in to them quickly and we went in to our routine. Frankie and I lugged cables and bags of gear in to the hall while John loaded up his trolley with mic stands, speakers, amps and his mixing desk. Within an hour we had the stage in the hall decked out with sound equipment ready for the band. John gets plenty of work but then again, he is the best sound engineer for miles around.

Frankie and I were on stage helping check the mics when the band came in.

'Hi, Dee,' one of them called to me across the hall.

It was Alec, a tall, thin lad with short, ginger hair; I'd seen him now and then singing with a few bands in the area. The rest were all new faces. The drummer had even more stuff than most and we all helped her to set up; she introduced herself as Stephie. She readily handed Frankie drumsticks to have a quick bash on her kit when she heard Frankie was a keen drummer too.

Having done our bit, we left John to do the sound check and we took the opportunity to get backstage and weigh up the band.

'That bass player ... Matt is it? He's quite good looking but a bit sleazy,' Frankie whispered.

'I think he might be with Stephie,' I said. 'What about Alec, the singer?'

'Full of himself,' she decided.

A few early birds had begun queuing and as soon as the sound check was over the janitor took pity on them standing out in the wind and rain and let them in. Alec, Stephie and the rest of the band came backstage. It's at this time that we usually leave bands to themselves; musicians can be a funny bunch, especially before a gig. But Stephie pulled out a few cans of beer and tossed us one each. It seemed I was right about her relationship status. The bass player wrapped his arms around her. 'We can always rely on Steph to come up with the goods,' he said, taking the beer from her hand.

'Stop mauling me, Matt,' she said. 'You only want me for my supplies.'

'And your sexy grooves, honey. No one can beat those skins like you do.'

Frankie raised her eyebrows in my direction and I nodded. It was time for us to leave, beer or no beer. We turned and waved our cheerios but Matt followed us out and caught hold of Frankie's arm. 'Not so fast, my wee, budding drummer,' he whispered. 'I would like to make your acquaintance further when we can be more private.'

'Nothing would give me greater pleasure,' she answered with a sarcastic smile, 'but Mummy always warned me about rock stars, especially those in the embryonic stage.' She tugged her arm free and linked me.

'What a creep,' she whispered as we left, loud enough to be overheard. You have to hand it to Frankie, she knows how to handle the boys. She seems to have an inbuilt GPS system to navigate around her love life but being tall and beautiful she has lots of practice.

We decided to head over to the local pub to wait in the warm and Frankie steered me through the hall where John was glued to his pedestal stool. Nothing would move him from his mixing desk until the end of the gig. Only when the gear was safely locked in his van would he allow himself an Irn Bru before driving home. He beckoned me over.

'Sorry I … I shouldn't have expected … didn't expect … Thanks for helping out tonight.'

'It's okay, we enjoy it. We get to meet such intellectual and witty individuals.'

'Dee, can we be friends again?'

'Friends is it? Like people who care about each other, look out for each other, trust one another?'

'You're still angry with me then?'

'I trusted you, John. I thought you trusted me.' I turned from him quickly so that he wouldn't see my eyes welling up with tears.

'How's the reconciliation going then?' Frankie asked as we nursed a Coke each in the warm, snug pub.

'What reconciliation?'

'You and John.'

'Frankie, you didn't arrange this tonight, did you?'

'I just thought it would be better if you were friends again. I don't expect you to get back together or anything.'

'But Frankie, he thinks I somehow got Amy in to that bin. He thinks I hate him. He probably thinks I went with Tom to get back at him.'

'Is he coming tonight?' Frankie asked.

'Who? Tom? Should he be?'

'A few of the gang are coming over. Has he messaged you?'

'You don't think he'll come tonight, do you?'

'So, there is a problem?'

'Not really...'

'Diary Night tomorrow,' Frankie said, holding me with those piercing eyes.

I nodded in agreement.

'And nothing held back, okay?'

I nodded again.

The gang fought their way through the heavy pub door. Sandi and Rhona looked as if they'd been arguing. 'I don't know anything about it...' Sandi was saying.

'Sounds like Rhona's extracting information about

other people's business again,' I whispered to Frankie.

Amy, however, was beaming fit to burst. She bounced up to us. 'I'm having a party Hogmanay. You will both come, won't you?'

'Need special invites, do we?' I said in to my Coke.

Frankie kicked me under the table. 'I'm sure we'll be there,' she said.

Amy started flashing a new mobile she'd bought in the sales. 'I much prefer getting money for Christmas, then you can choose your own model,' she was telling anyone who would listen. For once I considered agreeing with her.

I made my way to the bar for more drinks and I was joined by Alec who'd followed the gang in. He gave me a friendly smile.

'I'll get these,' he said to the barman.

'Mind if I join you,' he asked me, picking up the bottles and carrying them to our table. In one polished movement he pulled up a stool next to Frankie and leaned in to whisper in her ear. I saw her frown slightly. Again, he leaned in and whispered, this time picking up her hand and holding it in his. She smiled and gave a barely perceptible nod. The brief exchange over, he drained his bottle and left the pub.

'Not too full of himself then?' I asked.

'I might be prepared to see another side to him if he behaves in a gentlemanly fashion,' she conceded. We clinked our bottles together and giggled a Slainte.

'What's going on?' bleated Rhona.

The band was quite good. Not your usual bunch of show-off dead necks. A lively crowd filled the hall and I danced all night. Frankie was otherwise engaged as I helped John pack up at the end of the gig. My legs were aching and I was glad to pull on my trainers again. My hair was stuck to the back of my neck and I twisted it up in to a knot.

It took an age to load up the van and we began chatting together, just like old times.

Frankie stuck to her rule of not accepting a lift from a boy on a first encounter and joined us in the van on the way home. John dropped her first before taking me home. He turned off the engine and looked straight at me.

'Dee, can I see you tomorrow? Nothing heavy. I won't pester you; I promise. But it would be good if we could talk for a while, catch up with what we're both doing. I'll bring a picnic if you like.'

He knew how difficult it was for me to refuse a picnic. And he hadn't spoken a word to Amy all night.

I gave in. 'Okay, I'll come over at two o'clock.'

He let out a huge sigh and ran to open the passenger door to let me out. He hurriedly planted a kiss on my cheek before I dashed up to our front door.

It was freezing in the house and I went straight to bed. When I was safely snuggled down, I checked my mobile. There were two new messages. One was from Frankie giving a few extra details of her tryst that she'd not been able to share in the van; and one from Amy, reminding me about the Hogmanay party and giving me a new mobile number. I hesitated for a moment but then added it to my contacts. There she sat again, all innocently, at the top of my list.

There was nothing from Tom. Nothing since the call I'd refused to take almost twenty-four hours ago. Despite everything, I felt let down. I switched off my mobile and put it to charge. I was glad I'd been working rather than partying. The walls kept still when I lay down in bed.

I was also glad I didn't have a headache when mum came bursting in to my bedroom in the morning.

'Dee, get up quick. Jacqui's at the door. Says she wants to ask you some questions.'

Six

'In you come, Dee,' Mum called, as I hurried downstairs to the sitting room.

Jacqui, our local police officer, was perched on the edge of the sofa sipping at a mug of tea.

I sat in a chair opposite her while Mum stood beside me, one hand on the back of my neck.

'Don't worry,' Jacqui said. 'I only want to ask a few questions.'

I hadn't been that worried but now I was. 'What is it? Is someone hurt?'

'No, no. Nothing like that. I won't keep you long. I'm here to talk about Tom Higgins.' She placed the mug on the carpet, clasped her hands over her knees and leaned towards me. 'Do you know him?'

'Yeah, I know him a bit,' I replied, inching backwards in the chair. 'I think he's been around for a couple of weeks now. Why?'

'Can you tell me when you last saw him?' she said, ignoring my question.

'Sandi's party, on Boxing Day night.'

'But you'd met him before that?'

'Well I met him at the Christmas dance in Glenappin. We had a couple of dances together and he bought me a drink. Nothing more.'

'So you wouldn't call him your boyfriend?'

'Not at all. Did someone say he was? Why are you asking?'

'You might know that he's lodging with Mrs. Fraser at Home Farm. She phoned us today because he hasn't been back for the last couple of nights. No one we've asked has seen or heard from him since that party you mentioned. Have you heard from him at all?'

'No.'

'No calls or texts?'

'No, nothing.' My tummy churned and grumbled. I wrapped my arms around my middle.

'Did anything unusual happen at the party? Did he get in to any arguments or fights, do you know?'

I shook my head.

'And do you know where he went after the party?'

'No. I think I saw him leaving before I left with Frankie.'

'Was he with anyone when he left?'

I remembered the glance he gave back at the house when he walked away, pulling up his collar against the winter winds. 'No, he was all alone.'

'Right then. Thanks very much.' Jacqui stood up and straightened her jacket sleeves. 'We're trying to get in touch with Tom's father. Apparently, he's visiting some relatives in Canada but we've not managed to trace him yet. Hopefully Tom will be back safe and sound before we have anything to tell him. Just let us know if Tom does contact you.'

'I will.'

'He is over sixteen,' she went on, 'but we do like to keep an eye on youngsters when they come to work in the area.'

'Poor Mrs. Fraser,' Mum said as she closed the front door. 'She was so looking forward to having a lodger over the winter. She could do without trouble like this.'

'Poor Mrs. Fraser!' I spluttered. 'What about Tom? He might be slumped in a ditch somewhere, dying of hypothermia.'

'He's a young lad. More likely he's hiding under a downie sleeping off too much Christmas spirit.'

John was waiting for me outside his mum's bakery. His backpack was bulging and I saw a crusty, French loaf poking out the top. John's mum, a striking raven-haired Italian, had often sent us off with a picnic when we first started seeing each other in the summer. We'd walk to the duckpond, feed each other bits of yummy pies and cakes and wash them down with bubbly homemade lemonade. In the autumn, when it started getting colder, John would bring along a blanket smelling of croissants and strong cheese and wrap it around us.

John made a point of checking his watch as I jogged up, then gave me a grimacy smile. But still, he linked arms with me and we walked down our well-worn path.

There was an uncomfortable silence as we perched

on the wooden bench and picked at the food. 'You still busy?' I asked. I threw bits of crusts at the ducks as they waddled past.

'Yeah, busy enough. I'm missing you though,' he said mock punching me in the arm. 'Had to get a couple of oiks to help out on the bigger gigs. Got a big one in the New Year actually. Fancy helping? I'll pay you something if you want.'

I didn't need to think for too long. I've always enjoyed helping out on gigs. 'Yeah, let me know when.'

We chatted on as we ate. He was genuinely interested in hearing all about what I'd been up to, even all the boring bits that nobody else wants to listen to. And he made me laugh a lot, telling me stories about his visit to his dippy aunt, like when he was making dinner and nearly cooked the cat because it sleeps most of the time in the oven, which she never uses.

As we talked, we snuggled in closer and his eyes grew soft and sexy again.

'Dee, I won't take it any further than you want,' he said, reaching out to take one of my curls and twist it around his finger, 'but nothing would make me happier than to be friends with you again.'

I opened my mouth to speak but he gently placed his fingertips against my lips.

'Don't say anything yet,' he whispered. 'I want you to know how I feel about you. I've missed you so much.' He picked up my hand from my crumb covered lap and folded it in his. I closed my eyes briefly and remembered how exciting the feel of his hands around mine had been.

It was these gentle hands that had stroked my body and moved me to new places. But a tugging pain in my stomach taunted me with the memory of his readiness to believe Amy.

Running steps and raucous voices on the path made me quickly pull my hand free. Sandi and Rhona, out of breath, planted themselves on either side of us.

'Thank goodness ... you're here,' Sandi panted, throwing herself on to John.

'It was mingin,' Rhona added.

John jumped up, all gallant like, Sandi still hanging from his arm. 'What is it? What have you seen?'

'Jimmy Johnson kissing his dog,' Sandi shrieked and they both ran off again, giggling.

'Bonkers, your friends,' John muttered as he packed up the bag.

But then Sandi ran back to me. 'I'm sorry. It wasn't my idea. Don't let Amy know I've told you; she'll murder me.' She pecked me on the cheek and ran off again.

'Told me what, you haven't told me anything,' I called after her.

'What's she on about?' John asked.

'I wish I knew.'

Frankie arrived wearing a broad smile and carrying a large bottle of Coke. She threw her jacket at the coat stand in the hall and laughed when it fell to the floor.

I'd piled Doritos in a big plastic bowl and we took our snack upstairs to my bedroom.

Diary Nights had started when we met up to write

diaries for our primary school teacher. We did so much together it was fun to chat as we wrote about things like special treats to ice-skating, birthday parties and ceilidhs in the hall. As we crept through our early teens, we still wrote our diaries together, even though no teacher wanted to read them. More recently, we'd decided some things shouldn't be written down where prying eyes might find them. So then we became each other's secret diary, compelled to tell each other our secret hopes, exploits, concerns and misdoings. We were equally compelled to listen without judgement, only offering advice if asked for.

So, I faced an evening telling Frankie about what had happened with Tom at the party and about the spooky fears I couldn't shift about my new mobile.

We tossed a coin to decide who would go first.

'Tails, tails, never fails,' I chanted. It was heads. Frankie chose to go first.

'I, Francis Macgregor, will tell all my secrets to Deidre Walker, and keep her secrets safe,' she began.

She was full of her time with Alec.

'Just because a boy smiles at you doesn't mean you have to fall in love with him,' I reminded her.

'I'm not in love with him,' she mused, 'but I did feel comfortable with him. He's sweet and caring.'

'He certainly made some sweet moves with that mic stand.'

'He's quite different offstage. He even apologised for the way that freak Matt was coming on to me before the gig. Apparently, Matt always expects there to be groupies dropping at his feet. Alec doesn't know how Stephie puts up with him.'

'Alec is a lucky guy to have met you,' I said. 'So, when do you see him again?'

She kneeled on the bed to look out of the window. 'He did ask to see me tonight,' she said. 'He's away tomorrow, gigging until New Year but I told him I had a very important prior commitment.'

I winced, then whispered: 'Thanks.'

'So tell all,' she said, picking up my hand and examining my nails.

'I don't know where to start.'

'Start with Tom.'

And I did. I got everything all mixed up but with lots of patience and gentle questioning she managed to piece things together. She was less shocked than I thought she would be, and I was less embarrassed than I thought I would be.

'He didn't really do anything to you apart from the kissing and awkward fumbling then? Maybe girls go further, faster, where he's from,' she said.

I had to agree that no, he hadn't gone very far at all but that I had been scared.

'He wasn't like that when I met him at the dance,' I said. 'He was shy and kind. It was all so unexpected.'

'Maybe what people are saying about him made you more anxious.'

'Do you think I overreacted then?'

'No, definitely not. He's a stranger. You were frightened. You didn't want what he was doing and you had to stop him. And, thank goodness, he did stop.'

I flopped against her shoulder and breathed deeply, filling my lungs with her tangy fragrance.

'News from the village is that Tom is still missing,' she whispered. 'Police have started searching all the barns and outbuildings.'

'Do you think his disappearance has anything to do with what I said when—'

'I shouldn't think so. He's maybe gone back home for a few days.'

'Hmm, maybe,' I said.

We both dug in to the Doritos.

Then it was time to thrash out my sinister phone experience with Amy.

'I'm sure there's nothing in it,' Frankie pondered. 'Like I said – just a coincidence.'

She wasn't convinced by my nod in reply.

'So what's your theory then?' she asked.

'Well ... what if I've suddenly developed some strange powers? I certainly felt odd when I had that vision of Amy in the bin.'

'Odd, how?'

'Like a bang in my head ... Like a sudden burst of energy in every one of my millions of brain cells.'

'Maybe a fit of anger, remembering what Amy had done.'

'Or maybe the phone has some sort of control over me, maybe it's cursed,' I went on. 'Dad might have bought it from some dodgy bloke in—'

'Can you hear yourself?' Frankie interrupted me.

41

'You'll be wanting me to believe in Derren Brown next.'

'But strange things do happen. Lots of people experience paranormal stuff all the time.'

With a sly look she said, 'You could always try it out again.'

'You are joking,' I said. 'Amy did give me her new number.'

We both giggled but my giggling turned to uncontrolled laughter. My eyes hurt and I began crying; deep sobs shook my body. I was scared. Even Frankie's dismissal of all things supernatural couldn't shake my fears that I hadn't been in control when my fingers had hovered over Amy's name and hit the delete button.

Frankie held me close. 'It's okay,' she said, smoothing the damp hair from my cheeks.

'You're always so ... sorted. Not like me. I'm a complete mess,' I said.

'Not a mess. You're confused at the moment.'

'Ha! At the moment? I live my life in constant confusion. You always make the right decisions – I never do. In fact, I rarely make any decisions. Life just happens to me.'

'Not so. You broke off with John.'

'And I'm not even sure about that. Was I too hasty?'

'You don't need to rush in to answering him. He's missing you; I think he wants you back.'

'But why? My hips are too big, my boobs are not big enough, I've a foul temper and I never stick at anything for more than two minutes. Whereas Amy—'

'Enough! No more self-pity,' she said. 'You're worth

ten Amys.'

'Good job her mum loves her,' I snivelled.

'Now, what about my eyelashes? Get your curlers and let me try out that new mascara.'

It was always good to share problems with Frankie and I went to bed more relaxed than I'd been for the last couple of nights.

But it didn't last long. I woke suddenly from a dream where I was being chased around the woods behind our house by a huge dog. I ran wildly in all directions but it reappeared, emerging from behind trees no matter which way I turned. Then, ahead of me, Tom was hurrying away, his feet snagging on rocks and fallen branches. I tried calling out to him but my voice wouldn't work. He ran further and further into the darkness until I couldn't make him out amongst the undergrowth.

It took a few moments for me to come out of the dream, and in the darkness of my bedroom I broke out in to a heavy sweat as I remembered deleting Tom's name from my phone the night of the party. 'Oh no,' I howled in to my pillow. What if deleting his name had caused him to disappear?

I had to find out what had happened to him. I remembered that he'd tried to call me a few hours after he'd left the party. I needed to know why.

Seven

Mrs Fraser wasn't pleased to see me when I banged on her door the next morning but she hung up my rain-soaked jacket, led me in to her steamy kitchen and within a few minutes I was sitting at her cluttered kitchen table with a cup of milky coffee. A ginger cat sprang onto my lap and purred deeply, digging its claws in to my leg. The kitchen clock, in the shape of a brightly coloured cockerel, emitted a brisk tick.

'Young people,' she muttered as she crashed pots and pans around, 'and police in and out all hours of the day.'

'Did Tom talk about where he was going?' I asked.

'Do you think I haven't told the police all of that? What youngster ever tells you anything that makes sense?'

'Did he take his phone do you know?' I asked.

'No, I don't know. It could be in his room. Go up and see for yourself if you like. The police had a good look around but you're welcome to. Mind your head as you go upstairs, that policeman nearly brained himself.'

At the top of the stairs I edged around the door to the spare bedroom, reluctant to go in to Tom's room without him knowing. It was quite gloomy with only a small window in the sloping roof overlooking the back yard. I watched a few hens peck around in the mud. Tom hadn't much stuff lying around: a few neatly folded t-shirts on a chair; a couple of music magazines on the bedside cabinet.

The single bed had been made since he'd last slept in it but the covers were scrunched up, like someone had been lying or sitting on top. His phone charger was on the bedside cabinet, still plugged in but there was no phone. I switched off the charger at the wall then took a look under the bed. There was nothing to see from where I was standing but I was still curious and I squeezed in between the bed and the wall. Something poked out from under the pink, flowery pillowcase. I pulled out a dogeared local map, folded over to show our village. In the top right hand corner someone had drawn a small cross in red ink. I squinted at it. It didn't mark anything in particular, just a part of the hillside, miles away from anywhere. I decided to take the map with me. I folded it and stuffed it in my bag.

Back downstairs, Mrs Fraser was standing by the kitchen window, absentmindedly stroking one of the tabby cats and staring out at the same hens I'd watched from upstairs.

'He was a nice boy all the same ...' she started. I wasn't keen on her use of the past tense.

'Do you think he's gone back to his family in Sunderland?' I asked.

'He's no close family there, dear. His dad's gone off

to Canada, probably on some wild goose chase. No ... No point in him going to Sunderland.'

'There was a map upstairs ... Do you mind if I borrow it?'

'One of Tom's is it? He always had his head in one map or another. You can bring it back if they find him.'

'When, not if,' I wanted to shout. I couldn't take any more doom and gloom. I thanked Mrs. Fraser, put on my jacket, pulled up my hood and stepped back out into the heavy rain.

I stood in the bus shelter for a while trying to piece together the few scraps of information I'd gathered: Tom probably had his phone with him but not his charger – so no more calls or messages after all this time then; it looked like he hadn't been back since the party so would only have with him what he'd had that night, which was not much if he was sleeping out in the middle of winter. And there was the map. I took it out of my bag and refolded it the way I'd found it, with our village in the centre and the small red cross in the corner. Although the point marked was nowhere near any roads, there was a crofter's track quite close by.

All well and good being the amateur detective but what next? I could take the map to the police, pass it over to them. But they'd want to know why I was prying around Tom's room. And if I started going on about my phone ...

There was no alternative. If it was my fault that Tom was missing, it was up to me to find him.

I leaned back on the thin rail in the bus shelter and closed my eyes, imagining how it would be to see Tom again and what I might say to him. I nearly started walking back home. The thought, 'what do I care,' claimed some attention but I opened my eyes and stared at the map again.

And as I stared, the brown contour lines began to fill out with slopes and hollows; gushing flumes of water surged through gorges; tufts of heather and browning bracken clothed the hills. I was like an eagle, soaring above the landscape. And I saw knots of people moving about: men and women were cutting turf, shifting stones, ploughing the soil; young women with infants strapped to their breasts were stooping over an enclosure, tending sleek, white goats; wee toddlers were chasing each other. A soft drizzle blanketed them all. And around each person, as if drawn by a child outlining the figures, a translucent, pearly sheen glimmered in the mist.

I circled wider, and saw low, stone buildings with black roofs, their edges made indistinct by smudges of smoke. And Tom was standing amongst them, isolated, invisible to them, or ignored. He stood with his back against a large white rock, his hands behind his head. I called out to him but my voice was a plaintive cry that merged with the sound of the wind whistling through the grasses. Then my head hit the Perspex sheeting of the bus shelter behind me and the image disappeared. It was a while before my eyes could focus on the yellowing timetable pasted on the wall opposite and the familiar graffiti scratched in to the plastic.

Was I seeing ghosts? It felt rather that Tom was merging with an image of a time past: a time when people survived by subsistence farming on the crofts; a time before the people had left.

I didn't stop to question why or how I'd seen this vision. The only thing in my head was that I'd ignored Tom's call; I'd deleted his name from my phone. Wherever Tom was, whatever he was doing, I needed to find what was marked by that red cross.

The clatter of rain on the bus shelter eased off.

I traced out the route on my mobile and set off out of the village. The first part was along a forest track which was quite dry underfoot. Shaking down my hood, my hair started to dry and bounce around my face. I quickened my pace, feeling better for doing something.

Eventually I left the dense forest block and came out onto the open hillside. With no pathway now, I needed to cross over rough ground to reach the croft track. The sky widened as I climbed higher and I saw the rain-blackened clouds chasing away. Crossing between clumps of heather and boggy pools slowed me down. I checked the time on my phone. It was taking me longer than I'd thought but I wasn't put off. I had another look at the route; it didn't look too far to the croft track.

My phone gave a bleep, alerting me that I was back in range of a signal. Surprisingly, I didn't feel comforted. My pulse quickened. Was I prepared for what I might discover? But I could only go on; retracing my steps was not an option. A stone wall covered in soft, green moss led me to the croft track. Another quick check on my mobile told me I was getting close to the marked spot. Nothing ahead appeared unusual or out of place, only a small copse of bare branched trees interrupted the skyline. Yet the exposed hillside felt threatening. I was alone. There was nothing and nobody around for as far as I could see.

I carried on along the croft track through the copse, the wind whipping up the dead leaves lying around. I came out from the trees and found myself standing on a small craggy summit. The stiff wind made me shiver. It was a great view, down to the village in one direction and out over the loch to the sea the other way.

The path turned sharply to the right. To my left, only a couple of steps away, was a steep drop. I peered down the slope. A large white rock erupted from the ground a little way down.

A person was crouched close to the rock.

Eight

I slithered down, grabbing at clumps of heather as my trainers slid beneath me. I caught hold of a sapling which stopped me slipping further.

Tom was crouched by the boulder, his hands covering his face. He looked solid and real, not part of a vision this time. I don't know if he'd been crying or maybe the wind was making his eyes water but when he stood up, he wiped his eyes with the back of his hands and reached out to me. I hesitated, remembering how his hands had ranged over my body but I let him help me regain my footing.

'What ...? How did you know where I was?' he said, shaking his head.

I pulled out the now soggy map and he nodded with comprehension.

'Is this the place on the map then?' I asked, panting to get back my breath.

He nodded again.

'Good view,' I said. Relief flooded through me. He was safe and, apart from the red blotches on his face, he looked well. But along with the relief came a dread. Despite Frankie's earlier words which had given me some reassurance about him, I was alone with this boy, miles from anywhere, and no-one knew where I was.

He gazed at me for ages, not blinking, not moving a muscle in his face. Then, 'Can you trust me?' he asked. He didn't wait for an answer but holding on to my hand he turned to climb back up the slope, pulling me behind him as my trainers slithered beneath me.

At the top he pointed to a low, stone building huddled beside a burn in the distance. The croft track wound away towards it.

'Come with me?' His voice was low and calm.

There seemed little point in refusing. 'Yeah. Okay,' I said.

All the important questions faded away as I followed Tom to the bothy. The once green painted door was falling from its hinges and Tom had to yank it a wee way open to let us squeeze in. The floor was trampled earth with a few broken stone flags here and there. A sour smell, like when you lift tatties from the cold soil, hung in the dank air. Dark green ferns grew on the walls where streaks of light fell from the gaping windows.

Tom strode over to a wide fireplace on the far side of the room. He scraped the embers of a fire together and placed on a couple of dry sticks. A crackle as the sticks took added to the clamour of the overflowing burn rushing by outside.

'How do you know about this place?' I ventured in

to the gloom.

'Roamed all over these hills since I was a kid. Know them better than you probably.'

'But how? You didn't live around here or go to school here. I would have known you.'

'There are more ways of getting an education than going to school,' he muttered in a way that put a stop to my questioning. He'd asked for my trust and that would have to be enough.

'Don't think much of the decor.' I laughed feebly, shaking some sacking hanging from a nail on the wall.

'Suits me,' he replied.

An ancient iron bedstead stood rusting in one corner. A heap of browning heather was piled on it and a fleecy blanket topped that.

'You're sleeping here then?'

'Yeah.'

'What about all the bugs and things?'

'They're no worse than the ones you get in houses.' And then he laughed, a quiet but deep laugh that reminded me of when I first met him. 'They're a bit bigger, that's all.'

'But why are you here?' I said. He stared into the growing fire. 'I ... I'm sorry,' I went on. 'I didn't mean to be nosy. I can see I'm in your way.'

'No. Don't you apologise. I'm not very good at talking about myself.'

'Everyone's worried to death about you.'

'That I don't believe.' He swung around from the fire place, flames now flashing up the chimney.

'Well Mrs Fraser and the police—'

'The police! What do they want?'

'They're searching all around the village. I promised I'd let them know if you contacted me. I suppose you're a missing person. They're trying to find out where your dad is too, to let him know.'

'My dad ... but he's in Canada. What about my note. Why didn't Mrs Fraser read my note?'

'You left a note?'

He came closer to me. His face crumpled and he closed his eyes tight. 'That night,' he started, 'after I left the party where we ... When I got back to Mrs Fraser's I didn't know what to do. I packed a few things and left a note for Mrs Fraser on the fridge telling her I'd be back in a couple of days. I tried to call you. I wanted to apologise ... explain ... but you didn't pick up. I came up here to think, be on my own for a bit ... I didn't think you would want anything to do with me.'

'You wanted to apologise? For—'

'I was so stupid to believe ... I got it completely wrong.'

'Got it wrong?' I asked.

He nodded. 'Your mate said I needed this if I was to get anywhere with you.' He rummaged in his pocket and brought out a square foil-wrapped condom.

'My mate said—'

'Yeah, the one whose party it was.'

'Sandi?'

'Yeah. She was quite drunk though.' He hesitated before saying, 'She seemed to be handing them around.'

I shook my head trying to take in what Tom was

telling me. 'Sandi told you ... that you'd need that ... with me?'

He turned away and leaned his arms against the fireplace. 'I didn't know how to talk to you. You're so gorgeous. I didn't think I'd have a chance with you. But then you came in the car with me. I was worried that maybe you'd had a bit too much to drink ... I'm so sorry I upset you. I would never do anything to harm you.'

'What have I ever done to Sandi?' I said. I quickly took out my phone and crossed to the light from the doorway.

'What're you doing?' Tom asked.

'Getting Sandi to tell me what on earth she was doing.'

I brought Sandi up in my contacts list. I was livid. My brain boiled with her stupid, malicious interference. Then suddenly, instead of creating a message I hit delete. It was a moment before I realised what I'd done. 'Oh no,' I howled.

'What is it? Is there a problem?'

'No ... Yes ... Oh I don't know. I'm such a mindless imbecile. Now what'll happen?'

'It didn't send?' Tom asked. He looked anxious, shifting between the fireplace and the door as if not knowing which way to turn or how to deal with this rambling, incoherent creature in front of him.

'Send a message to Rhona. Yes,' I went on. 'No ... Frankie. I'll get Frankie to keep Sandi in. There are no big black bins in houses.' I fumbled with my phone. 'Aaahh,' I screamed. 'No signal.'

Tom hesitated for a moment, then slid an arm around my shaking shoulders. 'Is everything all right?'

He guided me towards the fireplace, pulled the rug off the bed and draped it around my shoulders.

'You're wet and cold,' he said quietly, 'come and get warm by the fire.'

'I need to get back, check everything's okay.'

'Soon.' His voice was deep and warm like melting chocolate.

He folded some sacking on the floor and I hunkered down with my chin on my knees. My mind in a spin, I watched in silence as he rearranged the burning sticks and set a camping kettle on the fire. He added a handful of what appeared to be soggy grass.

'Nettle and rosehip tea,' he explained. 'One of my dad's favourites.' He took an empty jar from a shelf, blew across the top of it, then from a rucksack next to the bed he fished out a jar of honey and a mug. Within a few minutes I was wrapping my shaking hands around a mug of very strange tasting but quite enjoyable tea. My hands began to relax and my brain cooled.

'My dad is rarely home,' I said. 'I haven't a clue what his favourite tea is.' I sipped the hot pungent liquid. My heart had stopped thumping in my chest and my curiosity got the better of me. 'Will you tell me some more about your dad?'

He drew his fingers through his black hair as he considered it. 'Dad was from a travelling family,' he started. He gave a quick glance at me, checking my reaction. 'He went to school now and then.'

I stretched out my legs. 'Go on.'

Tom shuffled his feet on the cold floor then came to sit beside me. 'He met and fell in love with my mam at one of those schools,' he said. 'Then I was on my way.' He looked up with a defiant glint in his eyes but I wasn't going to judge his parents for what had taken place.

I reached out my hand and placed it on top of his. His look softened and he went on. 'Mam's family helped them set up in a flat together in Sunderland. They didn't have any more kids. Dad used to bring me here when he came to collect whelks.'

He set the glass jar filled with the browny-green liquid on the ground. I kept quiet, searching his face as his eyes flickered around the shadows. He smiled briefly, as if at some private scene only he could see. But the wavering smile was replaced by a look of deep sadness. He turned to look at me.

'Then Mam fell ill. She died. I was seven. Dad went to pieces for a while. He couldn't cope on his own but didn't know how to ask for help. We had a van and spent more time travelling, some of the time around here. But he'd promised Mam he would see that I got a decent job and that made him get back on his feet again.

'I'm so sorry – about your mam,' I said.

The corners of his mouth drooped and he took a deep breath. 'I'm on an engineering training course, and when this placement came up on the hydro-scheme I knew I'd have some cash to look after myself for a while,' he said, smiling a bit again. 'Some of Mam's relatives live in Canada. They are always pestering Dad and me to go and see them so I persuaded Dad to take the chance to go while I'm here.' Tom picked up his drink and took a large gulp before saying, 'Although Dad is much of a loner, family is important to him.'

'So, in a way you belong here too,' I said.

'More so than you know – not that you would think it from the welcome some of your mates gave me – Mam's grandparents stayed around here.'

I couldn't answer. I'm not sure I would have treated him any better than the others if I hadn't thought he was so good looking.

He went on. 'Dad used to make brilliant kites. I'd paint animal faces on them and we'd fly them up here.'

'I saw them!' I said. 'I remember watching them. I thought it was holiday-makers.'

His face broke in to that heart stopping smile. 'I used to see you on the shore, your curly hair flying in the wind. You looked so happy with your friends. I wanted to come and play with you. But my dad was right, wasn't he? You wouldn't have wanted a playmate like me.'

My shoulders stiffened as I considered his words. 'I need to go,' I said, even though I was reluctant to leave the warmth of the fire and the strange stirrings in the pit of my tummy.

'Will you come again?' he whispered.

'Here?'

Excitement bubbled up in my chest but while I was thinking how to answer he said, 'No, why would you?'

'Yes, I will. I'll come tomorrow. I'll bring something to eat ... if you don't mind?' I was still unsure how to talk to him.

'Sounds great. I'll meet you on the track above the rock. And if you bring some milk we can have ordinary tea,' he said and laughed.

'That rock's important to you isn't it?'

I thought I'd gone too far this time but again he smiled and nodded. 'You're getting to me, Deidre Walker.'

'Friends call me Dee,' I said.

'I know but Deidre is more romantic. Like some Gaelic heroine.'

I gave an awkward laugh. I was flustered and my hands were shaking again.

'Come on, I'll show you a shortcut back down,' he said.

The sky was clearer as we left the bothy but the sun was skirting the mountaintops, casting long shadows.

We ran together along the croft track but before we reached the copse of trees Tom came to a halt then disappeared down a narrow, deep gully. He held his hand aloft for me to follow him. I slithered down behind him, skidding on loose stones until we landed on a small cove on the loch side.

It was darker than on the hillside and rhododendron roots threatened to trip us along the way. As we erupted onto the shore, we startled a heron that was sitting crouched at the water's edge like a grumpy old man. Its large wings whirred through the twilight as it took off in search of another resting place. We followed a sketchy path along the stony shore until the lights in the village shone out a short distance away.

'Till tomorrow, Deidre.' Tom said, making it sound more like a question.

'Till tomorrow,' I replied in a small voice that kind of croaked on me, and he brushed my hand with his fingertips. Even in the shadows I could still see his face breaking in to that beaming smile.

As I went through our front door there was a familiar cinnamony aftershave smell. I ran through the hallway and into the kitchen shouting, 'Dad?'

'Good job I keep taking the iron pills,' he said as he lifted me off the ground in a hug.

'A few more grey hairs,' I said ruffling his untidy mop, 'but no disgusting nose hairs yet. You're still safe to be seen with.'

'That's good,' he said, 'because we're going for a wander after tea.' He went back to buttering a tall pile of sliced bread, before handing them on to Mum to put in the sandwich fillings. I groaned inwardly. I love going for walks with Dad but after the day's events I just wanted time on my own.

'Have you got a favourite type of tea?' I blurted out, 'You know, anything fancy, like rosehip or that kind of thing?'

'I do actually drink Earl Grey in the office. Why?'

'Thought I might get you some for next Christmas,' I said and he laughed.

I went in to the hall to make a few calls from the house phone while Mum and Dad made lovey-dovey sandwiches together. First off was the call to Mrs Fraser, with me telling her to look carefully on her fridge door. After a while of her searching, she came back to the phone, complaining that Tom's handwriting looked like a worm had crawled over the paper. Next, I called the police to say Tom was no longer missing and no, he was not back at Mrs Frasers yet, and no, I didn't think there was anything wrong with him, he was just staying away while he had a few days off work.

And lastly, the call I was dreading: was Sandi safe? Her phone rang out for ages but she eventually answered. She sounded muggy with sleep.

'Dee, how's it going? You comin' over? No official party tonight but a few of the gang are coming later on. Rhona's fixing a curry as we speak.'

'No thanks, Dad's home,' I managed to say. I wanted to spit out 'what made you do such a rotten thing to Tom the other night' but I was so grateful that she was still in one piece that I just said, 'Cheerie'.

It was dark outside, with only a slice of moon to give a bit of light. Dad carried a small torch that threw out a thin glimmer a few paces ahead but he only turned it on every now and then to give us an idea of where the road lay. We walked away from the house in silence, the looming trees at either side of the road a thicker black than the surrounding blackness.

'Now ... do you want to tell me what's going on?' Dad said. I was glad then of the darkness. 'Mum said she heard what sounded like crying last night with you and Frankie,' he went on. 'And she told me about the police coming around.'

'I'm always telling you what's going on,' I said, 'but you're never here to listen.'

'I am now,' he said, and I thought I heard a scrap of impatience in his voice.

'Where did you get my phone Dad?' I asked.

'What? Is it important?'

'It ... it might be,' I stammered. 'Was it a normal shop?'

'Very normal. Want to tell me why it's important?'

I didn't want to tell him but how else could I find out. 'Don't think I'm mad or anything but I think it might be making bad things happen.' And I told him of Amy's accident and how I'd imagined it before it happened.

'So you think that because Amy deserved to be stuffed in a bin your phone made it happen to her. Sounds like a neat idea to me. I might try it with my phone; there's a couple of blokes at work I'd like to dump in a bin.'

'Don't laugh at me, Dad, please.'

'I'm sorry,' he said.

'What am I going to do?'

'You mean with the phone?' he asked. 'Well don't worry; I won't take offence if you want to ditch it.'

Was it that simple? Could I just go back to using my old, considerably inferior but safe mobile? Put this new one back in its box and hurl it in the loch?

Dad put his arm around my shoulder. 'I must admit you've taken me by surprise. I was all ready to hear about you and John. Got my relationship counselling hat on and everything.'

'Oh, that's all over.' I even took myself by surprise at how definite I sounded. 'Do you remember when we watched that kite once when I was wee?' I said.

'I do indeed. I searched for ages to find one the same for you. Ended up buying you a Pooh Bear one. Not quite the same was it?'

'Did you know the people flying it?'

'Visitors, I think. A stocky man and a young black-haired lad. They came to the village now and then.'

'Tom. The boy's name is Tom,' I said, 'and he's visiting again.'

'Aha,' was all Dad said, and we walked back home.

Nine

'Will you tell me what it's like?'

'What what is like?'

'Being in love.' Tom lay sprawled across his 'homemade' cushions – hessian sacks filled with heather – the red glow from the fire giving a lustre to his slicked-back hair.

I wriggled on the fleecy blanket and leaned against the iron bedstead. 'I don't think I'm the person to ask,' I said. 'I'm barely out of nappies in the relationships game.'

'But you were in love with John.'

Somehow, throughout the morning, I'd spilled out all sorts of things about myself, including the whole story of me and John.

Tom tossed me another chocolate covered peanut, part of the wacky lunch we'd put together that had included a rather suspect stew with roots and leaves we'd collected earlier.

'Well I suppose it's like ... you can't think straight about anything. Your whole body is possessed, your tummy quivers like it's full of bubbles that can't help but rise up, and that's when you're not with them.' He looked at me – wanting me to continue. 'You spend all your time waiting for your phone to ring or a message to come and then, when it does, it makes matters worse; you read different meanings in to every word, and worry about what's not been said.'

'Sounds scary,' he said.

'Well there is the good stuff too.' I laughed, but I wasn't about to go in to more detail about that! 'What is scary though, is how all that can change,' I said. 'I spent nights swollen with pain after we broke up. I didn't think there would come a time when I wouldn't love John, and yet now, I still care about him and what he thinks about me but it just doesn't feel the same anymore.'

'Maybe you've outgrown each other?' Tom said.

'What do you mean?'

'I don't know, maybe we start to need different things from people? But hey, what do I know, I've even less experience than you. I've never been in love like that.'

I wasn't used to talking to a boy like this. I've only ever confided in Frankie but Tom did seem to make sense. Then it struck me.

'The other night at Sandi's,' I said. Tom grimaced. 'Is that something you are experienced in?'

'You mean sex?'

'Well ... yes, if you put it like that.'

He closed his eyes and shook his head. 'Not on my list of things achieved to date. Made a mess of it, didn't I?'

I felt like laughing with relief but I didn't want him

to think I was laughing at him. He'd gone to so much trouble to make the day special. It was a day so ordinary and yet so different.

It had started early. I'd surprised Mum and Dad by eating breakfast with them and then dressing, in their opinion, 'sensibly for the weather'. It was bright and sunny although the frost still had a firm hold of the outside world.

And when I'd met Tom as arranged on the croft track, in the morning sunshine, we were both bubbly with excitement. We dropped down the gully, and from the small bay beside the loch we walked towards the water, the sunlight hitting us directly in our faces.

Tom pointed out different types of seaweed. 'You can eat this one,' he said holding out some putrid looking, bright green slime that slipped through his fingers.

'No way are you adding that to our lunch,' I'd said.

That set us off, offering each other revolting things to eat. We scrambled over cliffs blanketed with frost and poked around in rockpools that we discovered we'd both poked around in as wee kids. We played sardines in secluded caves and chased over the beach.

When we'd exhausted the shore, Tom led me to a little-used path that wound up the hillside.

And as we climbed, we talked.

We talked about his dad and how he liked to travel about. And my dad and how he travelled about too.

We talked about his mam. And my mum.

We talked about living in a van. And about living in a house.

We talked about having friends. And not having friends.

And, like I said, as we wandered along, I told Tom all about me and John. About how John had one day taken his head out of his books and discovered I was someone he wanted to spend more time with. That was until Amy had interfered.

When we reached the rounded top of a hill, Tom stopped close behind me, sheltering me from the icy wind that was blowing. 'It was from here that I watched you playing on the shore all those years ago,' he said.

It was strange to think of him spending time so near to me, and yet inhabiting a world so unrelated to my normal village life. We were like planets orbiting around a sun, crossing paths but never meeting.

Further along the path we looked down over the village. 'There's my house,' I said, pointing it out in the row of cottages next to the village shop; the blue painted windows and the white walls as familiar as my own reflection.

'Do you like living here?' he asked.

'Yeah, most of the time. Bit of a drag getting in to town on only one bus a day but there's not much to go to town for anyway.'

We watched the village going about its business for a while: the traffic turning in to the shop, people walking their dogs on the shore, the oyster catchers calling out to each other then taking off as one and flying low over the water. The sun skipped over the waves.

'What about you?' I asked. 'Do you like staying

here?'

'Hmm, it's okay. I like the scenery,' he said looking into my eyes. I turned and stared at the deep blue sky to hide my embarrassment. The only clouds were the remnants of aeroplane trails, crisscrossing the sky like strands of wool.

The path led to the bothy but before we went to prepare our strange lunch, we took a detour to the derelict house that burrowed in against a dip in the hillside. More recently built than the bothy, the house looked similar to the other croft houses scattered about our township; but it was a neglected relative, the two pointy eaves of the upstairs rooms jutting from the cold, grey granite face like startled eyebrows shielding the empty eye sockets of the broken windows.

Tom poked around in the remains of the vegetable patch. There were no recognisable vegetables growing here though, no rows of carrots, parsnips or winter cabbage like at home, no cold presses of tatties or apples in storage. I wondered if Tom knew what he was doing as he collected a few green leaves and stems, and rooted about under the soil, pulling out strange shaped tubers. He put the 'ingredients' in to a cotton bag that he'd pulled from his jacket pocket.

We didn't go in the house but tested out a bench seat in the small porch where the wind had used its force to gain entry. The porch door was a few jagged planks scattered on the sparse grass, white tendrils of fungi and black masses of jelly moulds rotting it away.

I didn't need to ask Tom why he hadn't chosen to

shelter here. The stench of decay flooded even from the stone walls.

'I want to show you something,' Tom said, pulling out a piece of paper from another pocket. He unfolded it and showed me a sketch with names written on. His name was there at the bottom.

'Your family tree?' I asked. He nodded.

'That's my dad,' he said, pointing to the name Jimmy Higgins. 'And that's Mam.' He pointed again to another name, Dorothy Higgins. He'd written dates next to them. Just the birth date of his father but next to his mam there were two dates; the later one about ten years ago.

'That was when she died?' I asked.

'Yeah. I was seven. And Mam's mam,' he pointed to another name, 'died giving birth to her. Mam was brought up in this house by her grandparents for the first few years of her life.'

'What about your mam's dad? Where was he?'

'I don't know anything about him. But he mustn't have been much good. Later, when Mam was a toddler, her grandmother was forced to move back to Sunderland where her family was, taking my mam with her.'

We poured over the sheet of paper, tracing out the family lines, Tom helping me follow who was who. I couldn't get over the gap where his grandfather should have been, or the early deaths of his mam and his grandmother.

'But you said your dad was in Canada visiting your mam's relatives?'

He pointed to another name. 'That's Mam's

grandmother's sister. Her family moved away from Sunderland to Canada not long after I was born but they'd been good to Dad and Mam, helping them set up in a flat when I was due.'

I got confused with all the branches – I can barely tell the relationships between all my own aunts, cousins and second cousins – so I was glad of the sketch showing Tom's.

Then my tummy churned and it groaned loudly. Tom's face lost its gloomy look at that, and his slow smile became a laugh as he said, 'Come on. Let's make some lunch.' And we had set off back to the bothy.

It was cold and dark inside the bothy and I was beginning to regret not suggesting having lunch at the Bistro in the village but Tom soon had the whole place transformed. No light came in from outside because he'd covered over the gaping windows but the fire quickly filled the room with an earthy light and warmth. Tom threw on a few pine cones from a large mound he'd collected and it sent out sparks and crackles. He'd lit a large candle and it burned in a corner, emitting a steady glow. Neither time nor the freezing weather was part of our world inside the bothy walls.

So, we prepared and ate our lunch, using a camping pan on the fire, combining ingredients in more imaginative ways than any TV chef. And then we lazed about, chatting and staying quiet in turns and talking about what it was like being in love.

I was drowsy, basking in the warmth of the fire, watching

Tom's body curl and twist on his homemade cushions, when Tom suddenly jumped up. He beckoned me over to the corner and blew out the candle. A sudden chill hit me as a large rock caught in the sacking curtains and fell to the ground. Gruff shouts and high-pitched laughter sailed through the sickening gap in the wall. Tom signalled for me to keep quiet. I didn't need telling twice. He crept towards the door and looked out. 'They're going away,' he whispered.

I was shocked. 'Who are they?'

'Just folk who think it's fun to torment strangers,' he said.

'But they can't know who you are, or that you're here.'

'It's not that well hidden ... unfortunately, and some people have taken a dislike to me whether they know me or not.'

'What were they shouting?' I asked. I couldn't believe what I thought I'd heard.

'I think it was 'gypsy rapist' or something along those lines.' He spat the words out like sour fruit.

'But why would they shout such horrible things—?' I stopped myself and turned away, embarrassed, hoping he wouldn't think I'd spread stories about him. 'You don't think I said anything ...'

He came behind me and placed his hands on my shoulders, 'Not for one moment,' he said.

I turned to face him, 'I told Frankie. I was confused.'

'I know this is nothing to do with anything you've done or said.'

'You trust me that much?'

He didn't answer but took hold of my hands. Then he leant towards me. His hands tightened around mine and my tummy flipped with pleasure anticipating his kiss. But he frowned and backed away, holding on to my fingertip until the last moment, then he let my hands drop.

'Don't stay here any longer,' I said. 'Come back to Mrs Fraser's. It's not safe here.'

'It's no worse than I'm used to,' he sighed. 'But I am planning to go back soon, probably tomorrow; even I get fed up with my own company after a while.'

We didn't linger. We headed out, dropped down the gully and reached the sheltered bay. Tom insisted that I get home as quickly as possible and he walked along to the edge of the village with me. 'I'll watch you from here,' he said when we came close to the first streetlight.

I turned to wave a final goodbye. In the half-light I couldn't be sure but it looked like a gang of people was walking along the shore.

Ten

Back at home I wandered from room to room, too restless to settle to anything. Dad was in the shower and it smelt like Mum was trying out all her perfumes in her bedroom.

I kept going over what had happened at the bothy, wondering if Tom was safe and if I should be doing anything to help him. I messaged Frankie, 'can you come over? I need to talk.' It was just sending when the front doorbell rang and I opened it to Frankie. She rushed up and hugged me. 'I'm so sorry,' she said. 'Does Tom know who it was?'

'How do you know about it?' I asked.

'Rhona just messaged me. She saw Tom going to Mrs Fraser's.'

'Oh, he's gone there, has he? We didn't see their faces,' I said. 'Well I didn't.'

'You were there too?' Frankie sounded horrified.

I told her how I'd been to the bothy and about the shouting and the rock being thrown in but that Tom had seen me safely back to the village.

'You don't know do you?'

'What?' I screeched.

'I think Tom's been beaten up. It must have happened after you left him. Rhona saw him limping up the lane with a bloody face.'

Then Frankie's phone received my message. She checked it, took a look at me and burst in to tears!

'I thought we'd go out for tea tonight, chaps. My treat ...' Dad was saying as he came lumbering downstairs towards us, stroking his freshly-shaved chin. He stopped short when he saw the state of Frankie and looked completely bemused. This was so unlike Frankie. I shrugged at Dad and pulled her up to my room.

'What is it?' I felt at a loss at this unusual reversal of our roles, in fact I felt like shaking her. 'Tell me ... What's happened?' But she was silent, apart from a few deep sobs. She wiped her face on a tissue I gave her.

'I just want you to be happy,' was all she would say. She zipped up her jacket which she hadn't even taken off, flew down stairs, rushed past Dad who was still wondering what was going on, and left the house.

I didn't know which way to turn, should I follow Frankie and try and get out of her what was troubling her, or go along to Mrs Fraser's and find out what had happened to Tom. I needn't have bothered worrying because Dad said, 'Go and get washed, we'll be leaving in five.'

'I can't go out with you when my friends are in such a mess,' I said.

He exploded at that, 'Can't you think about anyone other than yourself for a moment?'

'I just said I need to look out for my friends,' I spluttered.

'Your mother is upstairs putting on makeup for the first time in months. You're coming with us. No arguments.'

That didn't stop me messaging Frankie, and soon I received a reply from her, 'Will you give John a call? He won't contact you until he hears from you.'

I was quite grateful that I had to go to the bistro with the parents. The last thing I felt like doing was calling John. The meal out would buy me some time to think about what to say to him.

And when the message came from Tom, I was sitting eating Lasagne, listening to Mum and Dad gossiping about all the old biddies in the village.

'The moon rise will be brilliant, meet me at the bus shelter? xx'

'Think I'll pop and see Frankie,' I said pushing away my empty plate. 'If that's okay?' I aimed at Dad.

'No room for pud?'

'Nah, you're okay but only because I'm thinking of your wallet rather than my figure.' I slipped my jacket on and left the pair of them holding hands under the table.

'Just in time,' Tom said. He held out a hand and caught hold of me. 'Come on. We'll get a better view from higher up.'

It was then that I noticed Tom's face, a cut on his right cheekbone was covered with a dressing but the eye was puffy and almost closed.

'That looks sore,' I said.

'It's nothing,' he said. 'Mrs Fraser was in her element cleaning me up. She told me she used to be the nurse here.'

We left the bus shelter and climbed a wee way up the forest track.

'Frankie said—' I started. But Tom shushed me. We stopped and he nodded towards a cluster of Scots Pine trees silhouetted against a pearly glow in the sky. I shivered and he put his arm around my waist. The snow-drop-white moon began to rise from behind the hilltop, draping the surroundings with a silvery sheen.

'It's beautiful. Thanks,' I said and together we watched thin clouds slither across the sky.

'Frankie said she thought you'd been beaten up,' I finished this time. Tom shrugged. 'Do you know who it was?'

'I think I've seen them before but I couldn't say who they are. There was a couple of lads and a lass. Maybe they were showing off for her.' He carefully touched his eye with his fingertips.

'Was it the ones shouting at the bothy?'

'Probably. They must have followed us off the hill. I was walking back along the shore and they jumped out from the bushes. I was taken by surprise, otherwise I'd have got away.'

'Will you be able to describe them to the police?' I asked.

'Why would I bother telling the police?' he said. His body stiffened beside me.

'You can't let people go around hurling abuse at you and then beating you up. Stand up to them.'

'Don't you think I've gone through all this before?' His voice sounded weary. 'What will I tell the police? "They called me names?" There were no witnesses to say they set on me first. They would say I picked a fight with them. At least one of them will have a black eye too.'

'But you can't go on letting people push you around,' I persisted.

'I think I can decide what I can or can't do.' There was a cold edge to his voice I hadn't heard before.

'Why do you always have to run away from things? It seems to me that if anything happens to you, your answer is to run off.'

'And what would your answer be? Get someone else to solve your problems?'

I got mad at that. I turned away and started back down the track. Tom followed and we made our way in single file. The moon hung above us like a celestial goddess guiding us along, and as we passed through the trees, her light slanting through the branches made a lacy path for us to walk along.

As we reached the village Tom held out his hand to me and said, 'I'm sorry for snapping.'

'It's okay. I should mind my own business,' I said. I didn't take hold of his hand but I did follow him in to the bus shelter.

'Are you going back to Mrs Fraser's?' I asked.

'Yeah, I'm needed on the site tomorrow, and I could do with a long soak. I've collected my things from the bothy. Are you going to Frankie's?'

'Yeah, that's where I told Mum and Dad I was going.'

'Before you go ...' He kicked a few stones around and looked at the ground.

'What?' I didn't sound too encouraging. I was still mad with him.

'I picked up a letter earlier at Mrs Fraser's,' he said. 'It's from Dad.' He showed me a long white envelope.

'From Canada?'

'Yeah. He's having a good time by all accounts.'

He started taking out the letter, then changed his mind. He fumbled with the envelope and a photograph fluttered face down onto the ground. We both stared at the white rectangle on the grimy ground for a couple of moments, then Tom lifted it and blew across the surface before putting it back with the letter.

I could tell Tom wanted to say more.

'Will he be coming back soon?' I asked.

'I don't know. He's talking about staying there.'

'How long for?' I couldn't disguise my nosiness.

'Forever,' Tom said leaning against the graffiti covered wall. 'Mam's folks want him to settle down there with them. They have a massive farm. He'd be of use to them, helping out, fixing things, you know.'

'But what about you? He can't want to leave you?'

'No, he doesn't,' he said waving the envelope about. 'He's asking do I want to go too.'

Eleven

Frankie was just leaving her house as I walked up her drive. 'Rhona says the gang's at Le Club. Come on,' she said.

It was difficult to gauge Frankie's expression in the dark but I asked, 'You okay now?'

'Okay-ish. Alec messaged me to say he's away for Hogmanay. He was offered a load of money to sing for some fancy party. Did I tell you he was a Mod gold medallist?'

I could understand her being fed up with him being away but I couldn't help feeling she wasn't being completely honest with me.

'You didn't make a lot of sense before, when you were at mine. Is there something you should be telling me?'

'Did you call John?' she said, not answering my question.

'Oh no, I forgot!'

'How on earth could you forget?' She sounded exasperated with me.

'I was watching the moonrise.'

'What?' she exploded but she didn't ask any more questions.

We walked on in silence, each aware that we were holding something back. It felt odd. We've always shared everything.

There were loads of visitors in Le Club.

'Why do folk come to the Highlands to celebrate?' Frankie said, 'They'd be just as well staying home.'

'Ah well, it gives us a job cleaning up the chalets after them,' I mused.

Rhona and Sandi were in the pool room and after getting a couple of cans of Irn Bru at the bar we joined them. They were playing 'spot the new shoes for Christmas', which involved just that. They had got themselves in to a giddy mood and were giggling at any nonsense. Neither Frankie nor I could join in their hilarity, even when they progressed onto 'spot the new underwear for Christmas' which led to rather unpleasant observations and imaginings about the boxer shorts and thongs of the surrounding punters.

'What's up with you?' Sandi asked, and Frankie looked away. She looked close to tears again.

'I think we're both a bit tired,' I said and pulled Frankie into Le Ladies. She dabbed at her eyes and peered in to the mirror.

Without looking at me she said, 'Is your phone still misbehaving?'

'I dunno,' I shrugged. 'I know Tom's in a mess with

all that running off and getting beaten up but it was nothing that I saw coming like with Amy, and nothing's happened to Sandi.'

'Yet,' she said.

'What do you mean 'yet'?'

'I keep getting these horrible texts,' she said.

'Show me,' I demanded.

'I don't keep them!'

'Are they about Sandi?'

'Some are. Some are about Tom. Some are about both of them.'

'Both of them?'

'Yeah, and what they used to do together.'

'Sandi and Tom. Tom and Sandi? How? When?'

'They're just malicious.'

'Who are they from?' I had a chief suspect even then.

'Someone who knows them quite well, I think. Sometimes the texts say it's disgusting, them being cousins.'

'Cousins?' I felt like a parrot repeating everything Frankie was saying but I was having difficulty making sense of any of it.

'It looks like someone knows more about Tom than we do, and none of it is very nice,' she said.

'Do you think any of it is true?' I asked, 'If Sandi is his cousin, she's never said anything about it.'

'And she didn't know who he was when he first came up,' Frankie added. 'No. I don't think that bit is true,' she concluded.

'Why didn't you tell me about all this before?'

'They only started coming last night ... Plus, you've not been around much today,' she said.

'I was with Tom.'

'All day?'

'Pretty much.'

'And again this evening?'

'Yeah,' I answered.

'Bet your Dad's not very pleased.'

'Hmm.' She was right there. 'I suppose I should be getting back before he has any more to complain about.'

We both decided to head for home. We were picking up our stuff from the pool room when in walked Amy with Matt draped around her shoulders. They were followed by a bunch of surly looking lads.

'How's your mate?' Matt called over to me.

I chose to ignore him but one of the goons behind him called out, 'Not very polite these country hicks, are they?'

Sandi and Rhona looked anxious. Amy gave a nervous giggle.

I don't know where I found the courage from but I spoke up. 'I've got lots of mates. Who're you talking about?'

'Your new lover boy. I heard he's getting more than his fair share of the talent. You want to be choosier whose hands you put yourself in,' Matt sneered.

Then everything kicked off before I could tell what was happening. John had followed Matt's mob in to Le Club and had obviously heard their comments. Without a word of warning, he launched right in to them, fists flying.

A huge fight broke out, lads from the bar joining in to help John. Amy fled from the centre of it all and cowered by the pool table. Rhona and Sandi pushed back their chairs and were making for safety but they didn't get very far before a bottle, launched from within the fray, sailed through the air and caught Sandi on the side of the head.

She crumpled like a burst balloon and hit the floor.

Twelve

The fight stopped as quickly as it had started. Sandi lay on the dirty, threadbare carpet, a trickle of blood streaking across her face.

By the time Rhona had checked Sandi over, and Sandi had opened her eyes and pulled weird faces, there were blue lights flashing outside the windows and paramedics rushing in. The police were not far behind the ambulance and they got to work writing down the names of all the lads. The paramedics soon had Sandi cleaned up but decided to take her for a check-up, especially when they knew there was no-one at home. When he was allowed to go by the police, John offered to walk back with me, Rhona and Frankie.

'Not like you to start a fight,' Rhona said to John when we got out into the cold night air.

'I wouldn't say I started it,' he replied, sounding insulted. 'I couldn't let that slime-ball Matt and his cronies get away with badmouthing you all like that. I followed them up the road; they were bragging about another fight they'd been in earlier. Thugs,' he concluded.

We reached my house and I could tell John was torn between wanting to talk to me and honouring his promise to see us all safely home. Frankie could sense the problem too and said, 'Can I use your bathroom, Dee.' She pulled Rhona in to the house with her, leaving John and me outside the front door.

'Frankie said you might call,' he said.

'Sorry, it's a bit crazy today. And then Dad wanted a family tea.' I wasn't joking either. The day had been so jampacked I was convinced I lived through about two weeks' worth of normal life.

'I thought maybe you were trying to avoid me.'

I winced. 'Not avoiding,' I admitted, 'I'm just not ready to say much yet.'

'You know how I feel about you. I hate to pester you but I came out tonight in the hope of meeting up with you. Say you don't mind me coming to see you.'

I faced him in the moonlight. The same moonlight I'd shared with Tom a few hours earlier.

'Why should I mind?'

'Good, good ... and sorry about that commotion. I've never been keen on that Matt.'

'Do you know much about him? You said he was in a fight earlier today?' I felt pretty mean asking John for information like this but I felt sure the other fight must have been with Tom.

'Not much. But I know Frankie doesn't like him, does she?'

'Oh ... no ... I suppose not.'

We could hear Frankie and Rhona whispering on the

84

other side of the front door. John stepped towards me. He spoke quickly, breathlessly. 'Dee, you can be infuriating and pig-headed and I never know how you're going to respond; you often seem to wilfully misunderstand me. It can be like juggling with eggs being with you but ... I miss you.

Frankie made a big show of opening the door and Rhona coughed. Then they all walked on up the road, leaving me with John's words echoing in my head. Was I so difficult to be with, and did he miss me that much?

Mum and Dad were sitting together watching a movie and I joined them for a while, then I said, genuinely, 'I'm so tired; I think I'll go to bed now.' They muttered to each other about needing to get up early themselves to go shopping.

'Will you hang around in the house while we're out tomorrow?' Dad asked. 'I'm expecting a call.'

I grunted some sort of answer and went upstairs. I showered and rolled in to bed and was deeply asleep when I was woken by my phone's message tone.

'Sorry. Will you meet me?' Tom messaged me.

I didn't even think about whether to answer or not. 'Ok. When? Where?' I messaged back.

'Now. Outside.' He replied.

I peered out of my bedroom window but couldn't see anything or anyone. I looked at the time; it was half past two. I shook off my jammies and pulled on jeans and a fleece. There was no sound in the house, no light shining from Mum and Dad's bedroom. I crept downstairs. I'd never done anything like this before. I looked at the front door. Opening it would be noisy. My windup torch was on the hall table and I switched it on to make my way through the kitchen to the back door. Was Tom out there?

In the silvery light of the moon I could see him leaning against the wall. I smelled his outdoorness, fresh and sweet. He didn't speak as he reached his hand out towards me. I took hold of it and stepped towards him. Tucking our clasped hands behind his back he pulled my arm around him then wrapped his arms loosely behind me. We held each for a few moments, examining each other's faces, still neither of us speaking. We leaned in closer. His hair tickled my face. Then his lips met mine and he gave me a small, gentle kiss.

'You all right with this?' he whispered.

'More than all right.'

As we kissed again his arms tightened around me and my whole body melted in to him.

'Thanks,' Tom said.

'What for?'

'For meeting me, for forgiving me, for being beautiful ...' he said, stroking my hair. 'Would you come with me tomorrow?' he went on. 'I have to inspect the site but we could go for a walk as well.'

'I'd like that.'

'I'll meet you here then ... ten to eight. We'll get the bus.'

'Okay.' I chose my next words with caution. I was enjoying myself and I didn't want to get in to any more arguments. 'Tom, did you know Sandi before you came here?'

He studied me closely. 'I'd seen her around, like I'd seen the rest of you.'

'I'm not trying to be mysterious but Frankie's hearing some odd things,' I said.

'Like?'

'Like ... that you and Sandi are cousins ... and that ...'

'And what?'

'You got together some time...'

'I've no idea if Sandi is any relation to me. It's possible I suppose; she could be part of Mam's family.' He smiled at me. 'But the rest is fiction.'

'I didn't believe that you and she—'

'I know,' he said and kissed me again.

'About tomorrow?' he said after a deliciously long time.

'Yeah.'

'Can it be ... like a date?'

I laughed. 'It can. Our first date.'

'So does that mean we're going out?'

I tugged his hair. 'Yeah, we're going out.'

'Till later then,' he said, and this time it didn't sound like a question.

I pushed open the back door as Tom slid away in to the shadows. It was darker in the house than out in the moonlight. I swung my torch in a wide arc to negotiate my way through the kitchen and the thin beam picked out Dad standing by the kitchen table.

'And your explanation is?' he exploded in to the gloom.

Thirteen

Grounded! For the first time in my life, at the grand old age of sixteen. I've built up a good understanding with Mum, and we usually agree on arrangements to suit us both. Okay, sometimes I have to be home before other girls younger than me but it's better than hassle and arguments. But Dad!

'You're never here. And when you do turn up, you think you can lay down the law, regardless of what Mum might think,' I'd shouted when he'd turned on the kitchen light and wouldn't let me go back to bed until I'd 'explained' my 'creeping around the house at all hours of the night' as he put it.

'Tom wanted to ask me out,' I said, and it sounded quite reasonable to me. But not to Dad.

'Can't he call at a decent time of day?'

'He's a bit ... different,' I said. But that didn't go down very well either.

So, with the sun shining on another frosty morning, I was watching for Tom to come up the path. Dad had suggested that I tell Tom I wasn't able to go with him, for the sake of being polite. What I didn't expect was for Dad to come behind me and watch with me.

'I thought you were going to town with Mum,' I said. But Dad strode on towards the gate as Tom approached the house.

'Good morning, Tom,' Dad called. 'Are you going up to the site? Janice and I can give you a lift if you like; we're going that way to town. Dee needs to have a word with you first though.'

How embarrassing are dads? I thought my face would never return to its normal colour after that speech.

Tom was fine with me not going with him; he seemed to understand where Dad was coming from, and was grateful for the offer of a lift. What was even worse, when Mum and Dad got back from town, Dad said they'd invited Tom for tea. 'Do things in a proper fashion,' he said.

Tom was grinning like the Cheshire Cat when he joined us for tea. Mum had baked cakes and was revelling in having a visitor and Dad was acting like a spider on speed, talking to Tom about engines and valves and pumps, and darting around the house, bringing out grubby manuals and bits of rusty machinery. They only left us to ourselves when they went to washup in the kitchen.

'Your mum and dad are great,' Tom said.

'So great they kept us apart most of the day.'

'Maybe if I ask them nicely, they'll let us go for a walk just now.'

I couldn't believe it. Tom was acting like a regular

crewcut boyfriend. It felt kind of nice. Mum and Dad seemed equally pleased with him and even agreed to us going for a walk as long as we stayed in the village and I was back by eight o'clock.

We agreed to walk up to Sandi's. Frankie had messaged me during the day to say Sandi was doing fine and her mum and dad were back from holiday.

The jolly Santa was looking a bit battered but the flashing icicles were still keeping their beat. Sandi came to her front door, showing off a square white dressing on her forehead. Her mum had said she wasn't allowed out, so we joined her in the front room. Tom and I huddled close together on the sofa.

'Hiya,' Sandi said to Tom. 'Nice to meet ya.'

'Tom was at your party,' I told her.

'Aw right, so you were an' all. I never forget a pretty face,' she said and winked at Tom. 'You don't need to blush, Dee. Tom knows he's safe enough with me.' She didn't seem to have any recollection of causing ructions and I wasn't going to remind her.

Tom said, 'I'm sorry you got hurt last night; I hope you're feeling better.' Then, before she could even answer, he came right out and asked, 'Sandi. Someone thinks we're related. Do you know anything about your family history?'

Sandi didn't bat an eye but said, 'Mum's got loads a family stuff. She'll know.' And with that she called, 'Mum, get your butt in here, will you.'

Sandi's mum relished the chance to get out a biscuit tin full of photos and a giant family tree she'd drawn on a rolled-up piece of paper. After masses of questions and answers were batted to and fro, and the comparing of notes –Tom took out the paper showing his family tree – she pulled out a school photo and pointed at a shining teenage face. 'That's your mum, Tom. It was sent to us when she was at secondary school.'

He stared at it for a long time while we all waited in silence.

'She was my cousin's daughter,' Sandi's mum went on. 'I never saw her after her family moved away; we were both just bairns when she left. I heard she'd had a lad and ... and we were all that sad when she died. I'm sorry Tom; I wished I'd known you were here.' With that she gave him a huge hug. 'You must call me Aunt Anne,' she said.

'You didn't despise Mam then for what happened? Who she married?' Tom asked.

'What on earth makes you think that?'

'My dad being a traveller, and her being so young when she—'

'I don't know much about your dad but nothing was ever said against him in the family. All I've ever heard is how much he loved Dot, your mam.'

Sandi and I looked at each other. Tom was managing to hold back tears but both of us had wet faces.

Sandi's mum put a log on the fire and came back a few minutes later with hot chocolate and biscuits for us all. 'You can have a dram later,' she said to Tom. 'I'll fetch Mrs. Fraser and you can come for the bells.' Tom stammered his thanks.

Our reverie was interrupted by the doorbell and Frankie joined us in the living room. She looked bedraggled and cold.

'You look miserable,' Sandi said as Frankie fell in a heap on the floor by the fire.

'I'm fine, how are you feeling?' Frankie said and she passed Sandi a box of chocolates.

'Doc says I'll live but I've to stay indoors for a couple of days. Won't make Amy's party tonight.'

'Sandi and Tom have just discovered their mums were cousins,' I said to Frankie.

'So it's true then?' she asked.

'Seems that bit is,' I said.

Frankie didn't answer but stretched out on the floor, exposing her skinny belly.

My phone then gave a beep. 'On way to see Sandi. Let me know if you want a lift. John x' I put it back in my pocket without replying.

Then Frankie's phone gave its cheery tone. She checked it and put it back in her pocket without saying anything. In the past we would have shared the contents of messages without a thought. Was it another malicious call? Her face gave nothing away.

'You two an item then?' Frankie said. It wasn't quite a challenge but neither did she sound enthralled by the idea. Tom grinned and I took hold of his hand.

Harry Styles again alerted us all to another message for Frankie. This time she said, 'Dad's just settling Granny for the evening. He's calling here on his way back. We can drop you two off; it's coming on heavy out there.' I looked at Tom and he shrugged, leaving me to make the decision.

I was mindful of my curfew and I thought a lift would also keep me out of the way of John when he drove up but I wanted to spend more time alone with Tom, so I said, 'It's okay, I need a bit of a walk, I've been revising all day.'

'See you at Amy's then,' Frankie said.

'Probs. I'll message you.' I said, adding nothing about being grounded.

Frankie gave Sandi a hug and left. The atmosphere was flattened and Sandi looked tired. Tom and I got up to leave too. Sandi gave Tom a huge hug and talked about wanting to get to know him better. As she was seeing us to the door, the doorbell rang again. John and Amy were standing huddled in the shelter of the small porch. John was holding a bunch of flowers.

'John took pity on me and gave me a lift,' Amy said.

'It's coming on to snow,' John said, avoiding looking at me and Tom.

'Laters,' I said as I pulled up my hood. Sandi gave Tom another hug, then showed John and Amy indoors.

It probably wasn't my best ever decision to walk back home. The snow was coming on thick and it was already gone eight. But walking with Tom was fast becoming my favourite pastime.

We took the glow of Sandi's log fire with us and stopped short of my house to linger in the shadows and say our goodbyes before Tom slipped away.

As I got near the house Dad pulled open the front door, making a big show of looking at his watch. 'Thought you knew how to tell the time, Dee,' was my welcome home. 'I'm pretty liberal in my terms of a grounding I think; you should respect the limits and stick to them.'

I couldn't believe the fuss Dad was making. 'Dad, I'm less than twenty minutes late. I'm sixteen—'

'Yes, I know, and you could have left home and be fending for yourself. But you're not and your Mother and I are still concerned for your welfare. All this chasing around. Why can't you call and say where you are from time to time?'

'I was only at Sandi's. And Mum is perfectly happy with the way I am when you're not here.'

'Don't bring that in to it. Your mum and I want you to stay in tonight and that's it. If you can behave yourself, you can visit your friends tomorrow.'

'But it's Hogmanay!'

'Mum and I will be staying up for the bells. Frankie, or Tom for that matter, is very welcome to come here.' And with that he went in to the kitchen, letting out steamy smells of venison casserole.

I hurried to my bedroom, snuggled under my downie and started a message to Frankie. I was reeling with the injustices and needed to share with her. 'You deserve a better friend than me.' I scratched that and started again. 'I'm grounded would you believe! Will you come round?'

'You can't be serious,' I said.

Frankie was sitting hunched up on my bed.

'You did ask me what I thought you should do.'

'But finish with Tom, a day after I said I'd go out with him? I like him. Very much. He's fun.'

'There's been nothing but trouble since you met up with him. When were you ever grounded before? Why are you grounded now? All this bother only started since Tom came on the scene.'

'What are you saying? That Tom is somehow to blame for the fights, and for Amy and Matt being a nuisance? Just because his dad's a traveller? Is that it?'

'I'm just saying that things were fine, then Tom turned up and now they are far from fine. And we still don't know much about him, do we?'

'We know he's Sandi's cousin. Sandi's mum was all but ready to adopt him earlier.'

We both mulled over what she'd said. Frankie always talks sense but I didn't want to hear what she was saying this time.

'What about your phone? Any more funny messages?' I asked.

'Not since the fight at Le Club. Maybe whoever was sending them got what they wanted.'

'Has Alec called?' I asked, wanting to change the subject for a while.

'Yeah, he's in Dunoon,' Frankie said with a smile on her face for the first time in ages. 'Says he's had a wicked tour and can't wait to see me again. He's just got this one slot of singing then he'll be travelling back tomorrow with the rest of the band. He's got a few gigs around here after that.'

I couldn't help feeling pleased for her, even though she did seem intent on wrecking my love-life.

'Are you going to Amy's party then?' I asked her. It wasn't reasonable to ask her to stay with me.

'I thought I might, unless you don't want me to. Your dad won't change his mind, will he?'

'He's more likely to become a vegetarian than let me go out tonight.'

Frankie laughed at that.

'And you say Tom's going to Sandi's with Mrs Fraser.'

'For the bells, yes. But Sandi won't be allowed out to the party after.'

'I'll go and keep you informed,' she said. And I had to make do with that.

Dinner was good; Mum is an ace cook and Dad always appreciates what she makes. He'd chosen a special French wine 'to compliment the strength of the venison' he said, which I actually quite liked. I decided to play it mature but frosty. I wasn't going to let them think I was okay with being grounded but I had enough going on in my head not to add extra grief from the parents. After dinner, a few neighbours came around to be jolly on the last evening of the old year before going back to their own homes to listen to the bells bring in the New Year.

'I'm going to do a bit of school work,' I said to Mum, 'seeing as I have to stay in,' I aimed at Dad.

Ten minutes later, when Mum brought through a cup of tea and a huge slab of fruit cake to the living room I had two windows open on my screen. One on an essay

I'd started for English on the poem 'Resurrection' and another searching the internet for variations of curses and jinxes. I'm pretty adept at switching between windows when I hear someone approaching, and as Mum looked at the screen she said, 'Great poem, that. Remember when I went to see her perform not long ago? That was a real treat.'

We talked a bit about the poem and how poets choose their words with such care. 'Do you think she meant all these things people say about it?' I asked.

'She's a clever woman but who knows what meanings she wanted to provide a glimpse into. Just enjoy it anyway.'

I was enjoying the poem, and talking to Mum like this. Then she said, 'And what else is it you're looking at?'

I felt my blush then clicked on the web page. It was some weirdo chatroom describing paranormal experiences.

'Not your usual area of study.' She sounded suspicious.

I toyed with telling her more but the neighbours were getting raucous in the dining room, they'd probably started betting on the cards. 'I have to write a creative piece too. 'Write about a situation from the point of view of a character completely different to your own',' I read from a sheet that I pulled out of my English folder.

'Hmm,' she said. 'Well don't be too long. Come and join us before twelve. I've got some of that fizzy Lambrusco that you like.'

Fourteen

After half an hour or so ferreting around the internet I came across loads of sites about the paranormal and premonitions, about telepathy, second sight, curses and jinxes and ended up confusing myself even more. Lots of people consider strange happenings as quite ordinary and I discovered that my recent experiences were really not at all unusual.

What I did find though, was that some people either buy into the whole paranormal idea and will put forward loads of examples and offer lots of ways to help, whereas others will try and explain away any number of bizarre events.

I switched off the computer and sat quietly in the darkened room. I've never given a lot of thought to such things before. I found myself swithering between the two positions, one moment believing that something weird was happening to me, something I didn't yet understand, then next minute accepting what Frankie had said, that it was all a twist of events. Although I hadn't yet told her about my daydream: about seeing Tom merging with the ghostly people on the hillside. But I always came back to how I saw Amy in that bin before it happened. Was that just a coincidence?

Dad came in and hugged me. 'You're growing up so fast. Come on. The rabble have left; come and watch Phil and Aly.'

The three of us huddled close to the telly and sipped our drinks. At midnight we watched Mons Meg blast in the New Year in Edinburgh and the fireworks whiz in to the sky around the castle. Then Dad turned off the telly and we sang Auld Lang Syne together.

It wasn't long before the knocks at the door started and Dad ushered in a stream of visitors banging their feet to stamp off the snow.

I went up to my room to listen to some music and was actually falling asleep when my messages started arriving.

The first from Frankie: 'I'm off to Amy's. Will call in before I go back home.'

'Happy New Year Dee. See you soon, love John.'

'thanks for the brill new cus. HNY Sandi xx'

Then a knock at my door and Mum peeked around. 'Visitor for you, love.'

She opened the door wider to let Tom come in. Melting snowflakes glistened in his black hair but his face was quite still; there was no friendly grin.

'What is it?' I asked.

He took a couple of steps and perched on the edge of my bed.

'Has something happened? Something bad?' My

mind was still full of spooky stories from the internet.

Tom wouldn't look at me. He picked up Ted who was avoiding the whole situation by lying face down on the bed.

'I don't think I should see you anymore,' Tom said.

'What? Has Frankie said something?'

'So Frankie thinks the same, does she?' His voice was flat. None of his usual deep fluid tones.

'What Frankie thinks is irrelevant,' I said. 'Why are you saying this? I thought you liked me.'

When, at last, he looked at me his dark, witchy eyes locked on to mine. 'I do like you ... very, very much.' I instinctively reached out to him but he just held on to Ted. 'I can't imagine what you see in me though,' he said.

'You're fun to be with. I like you ... a lot. And you don't look like the back of a bus you know.' He relaxed a bit at that and sighed but he still didn't smile. 'You say you like me. Why should we finish?' I went on.

'Because I'm not the only one who likes you. And I'll be moving away soon, maybe even to Canada, and it's not fair to mess you around if you can be happy with someone else.'

'By someone else I suppose you mean John.'

He nodded. 'Sandi happened to mention how he feels about you still.'

I took Ted off him. Tom had squashed and squished him in to quite unnatural positions.

'John will always be a friend,' I said. 'We've known each other for so long; and yeah, we get on well. But it will never be the same again between us. Look.' I snatched up my phone. 'I'll message him, tell him there's no chance.'

Tom looked horrified, 'You can't do that by phone.'

'No, you're right. I'll see him later. Get things straight with him.' I edged closer to him. 'I don't want to think about the future; I want to live my life for now,' I said. I took him by surprise. I grabbed him by the shoulders and buried my face in his neck, breathing in his visceral odour. He became tense, his arms rigid. But I spread my arms over his and clasped both of his hands in mine.

'What do you want?' His voice came out kind of strangled.

'To spend time with you. That's all.' My head found a comfortable space on his chest and I snuggled in.

Tom relaxed a bit and we folded limbs around each other. A burst of loud music blared up from downstairs. 'They're on to the golden oldies,' I said.

'Shall we join them?' Tom said, although he didn't make a move.

My pulse was racing and I was beginning to wish that Tom was less of a gentleman as he kept his hands safely around my waist. 'That's probably a good idea,' I said.

A moment later a message came on my phone, 'no fun without you and Sandi. Amy's taken up with those losers that came to Le Club and Rhona's in a mood. I'll be over in a mo. F'

Dad was playing host by the table full of bottles, sandwiches and cakes. He passed us both glasses with amber liquid in.

'Whiskey, ugh,' I said, and emptied mine in to Tom's glass but I helped myself to some more Lambrusco.

Then everyone started forming long lines up the middle of the carpet and Mum shouted, 'Let's party!' Madonna came over the stereo and Tom pulled me in to a line. Scarily, he knew all the moves.

'It's a Sunderland thing,' he shouted above the racket, waving his arms like a cowboy throwing a lasso, and kicking out his feet.

Dad was still shepherding people in and the next time he went to the door Frankie appeared, banging her thin arms around her body; Alec followed her with a pair of snow-covered boxer-shorts on his head. 'They're clean,' he shouted. Then Rhona shuffled in with her duffle coat hood still pulled up, squinting through her steamed over glasses.

'I thought Alec wasn't back till tomorrow,' I said to Frankie.

'I just found him outside. He hitched a lift with a biker coming over tonight. He's mad,' she yelled.

'Mad to see you,' Alec said. Frankie flung her arms around his neck and they danced off around the room.

For once, Mum looked worse than I felt. Dressed in her fluffy pink dressing gown and the soppy poodle slippers I'd bought her for Christmas, she came in to my bedroom carrying a tray with cups of tea.

'Never let me drink more than three glasses of wine ever again,' she groaned, shaking her head.

Frankie was squashed up against the wall next to

me in my bed – it would need more than a cup of tea to revive her – and Rhona was curled on a pile of cushions on the floor.

I felt reasonably okay, no worse than what a good plate of rashers couldn't cure. I was pleased to smell that Dad was busy cooking breakfast.

'That was a good night,' Rhona said, pulling on her jumper and sipping her tea. I opened the curtains and looked out onto a glistening, white world. The sun slanting through the trees made sparkling jewels on the snow-covered branches.

Rhona picked up her mobile and flicked through the pictures, 'You're really in to Tom, aren't you?'

'Show me?' I asked and she passed it over. The picture showed me and Tom standing in a corner of the living room, our arms around each other, me with a wide grin and Tom obviously laughing out loud.

'Yeah, I really am,' I said.

'What're you going to do when he goes back to Sunderland?' How does Rhona always manage to ask the questions you don't want to hear?

'We're taking it one day at a time. Why worry about what might or might not happen?' I said as calmly as I could.

'Well I wouldn't let myself get in so deep without thinking about the tomorrows.'

I passed the phone back without looking at the other pictures.

'I'm going out soon,' I said, picking out warm clothes to wear. I needed to finish things properly with

John before I saw Tom again. I didn't want any obstacles between us.

Accompanied by a loud snore from Frankie, Rhona set off downstairs with the tea cups.

Fifteen

The sun was almost warm on my face as I kicked up snow with my wellies and walked through the village towards John's house. The first of my scheduled visits for the day.

His mum was pleased to see me. 'Ah bellisimo, my beautiful first footer,' she said, pulling me to her and planting three kisses on my cheeks. 'I'm making coffee, come in to the kitchen while I pour it out. You can take some to John. He hasn't surfaced yet.'

The welcoming aromas in her well organised kitchen wrapped around me and within a few minutes she had a tray prepared with two tiny cups of delicious smelling espresso and a plate of thick sliced panettone set on a creamy white lace cloth. It had taken me months to get used to the biting coffee she served; I was going to miss it.

I went upstairs, rested the tray on the antique table on the landing and tapped on John's bedroom door. There was a groan from inside the room, the door eased open slowly and John's face appeared.

I was scared to pick up the tray again, I felt sure I'd drop it. Suddenly, I didn't feel so prepared for what I was planning to say and do.

John opened the door fully and I went in. While he pulled on a t-shirt and jeans I turned away and put the tray down on his desk. He crossed the room quickly, smiled and kissed me briefly on both cheeks. 'Happy New Year, Dee.'

'Yeah, thanks ... and you,' I said, feeling a blush rush up my face.

'You didn't make it to Amy's last night then?'

I couldn't tell him I was grounded. He would want to know why and I didn't want to mention Tom's name. 'No. I stayed home, with Mum and Dad, you know.'

'Your dad's well?'

I nodded.

'And your mum? Maybe I could call by and see them later.'

'Uh ... well. I'm not so sure.'

He looked at me grimly, 'Dee, did you come here to tell me ...?' His face drooped and he held out a hand hesitantly towards me. I couldn't take hold of it and he dropped it again, lifeless by his side. He wasn't making it easy for me.

'You asked me ...' I started. I couldn't say any more. John's wounded face lessened my resolve.

'It's not good news is it?' he asked.

'John, I'm sorry,' I said.

He crumpled onto the bed. 'I was such a fool,' he mumbled in to his chest, 'and now ... how can I compete against "the rugged stranger"?' he said, looking up at me.

'It has nothing to do with Tom.' John winced at the

name. 'Well not entirely.' I sat next to him on the bed but I couldn't look him in the eye. 'I won't deny that I do like him but I wouldn't have given him a second glance if you hadn't pushed me away.'

'You still can't forgive me for being a brainless idiot.'

'I can forgive you. I make stupid mistakes myself ... all the time.' But I knew I'd never forget the pain he'd caused me. 'I just don't want to get caught like that again.'

'It's not serious with him then?'

'I don't want to talk about Tom,' I said. 'But I want you to be clear about how I feel about you and me. I ... I don't want us to get back together.' There. I'd said it. 'But ... we, we're still friends?'

'Yeah, okay ... whatever you want,' he muttered. He slid off the bed, ruffled his hair, hitched up his jeans and brought over the tray. I didn't feel like staying but I drank the strong coffee and picked a corner off the cake.

'When does he go back?' John asked as he saw me to the door and I stepped back in to the snow.

Why was everyone asking me the same question? 'End of the month I think.'

'Okay ... I can live with that.' And he closed the door on me. Closing off the warmth and comfort I'd become used to without realising it.

The snow had been cleared from the path up to Mrs Fraser's door. Tom's work no doubt. A ginger cat pressed against the porch window. I shivered as I knocked on the door and took out the piece of cake Mum had trusted me to deliver.

'Come on in. Quick.' Mrs Fraser closed the door behind us and pulled across a heavy velvet curtain. She nudged another two cats out of the way.

'Mum sent this,' I said. I held out the cake wrapped in cling film, the thick white icing mimicking the frosty piles of snow outside.

'Thank her for me, won't you. But I doubt you're here to see me,' she said with a knowing look. 'He's upstairs. Been as good as gold he has ... since that misunderstanding.'

I was nervous about seeing Tom, and as Mrs Fraser closed the kitchen door the staircase fell in to semidarkness. A patch of light from a high window shone on to a few of the stairs near the top landing. I took the first two stairs and hesitated. A shadow appeared above me. Tom stood at the top, looking down. Then he grinned at me and rushed down, two stairs at a time. If he hadn't caught hold of me, he would have knocked me back down into the porch.

'You're here,' he whispered and kissed my hair behind my ear. I shivered again but this time it had nothing to do with the temperature. He held my hand and climbed the stairs, pulling me behind him.

We turned in to his room and he let me sit on the bed. He pulled the wooden chair from the small desk, sat on it and gazed at me intently.

'Tell me what you've been doing this morning. I want to know everything,' he said.

'Well ... I've eaten three crispy rashers and some leftover sandwiches—'

'Nice.' His eyes shone wickedly at me.

'... washed some glasses, argued with Rhona ... and ...' I lowered my voice. 'I went to see John.'

'Oh,' he said and he crinkled his brow. 'What happened?' He straightened up in the chair.

Tom's expression changed several times as I told him what I'd said to John.

'He wanted to know when you were leaving. I told him I thought you'd be here until the end of the month.' Then my voice cracked as I asked, 'Is that right?'

'It's one possibility,' he said, his voice barely more than a whisper.

'There are others?' I hadn't forgotten the suggestion of him going with his dad to live in Canada. Was he planning to leave sooner?

I glanced at the desk. A photograph was propped against the table lamp. I guessed it was the one that had fallen in the bus shelter. What looked like a large family group was standing in deep snow outside a wooden building. There were people of all ages, some with arms around each other; some holding babies or toddlers.

'Is your dad in the picture?'

Tom lifted it and pointed to a dark-haired man. He looked smaller than Tom; his face was shadowy with stubble.

'He looks quite scary,' I said.

'He's as daft as a brush.' Tom picked up a sheet of paper from the desk. 'I was just writing to him, filling him in with all my news. I'm telling him how I've met this fantastic girl.'

Even though the temperature in the room was barely above freezing, the heat ran up my face as I blushed. I was saved from further embarrassment; Tom's phone received a message.

'We're going to meet my great-aunt,' he said and showed me the message from Sandi.

'There we are now,' Sandi's granny said as she welcomed Sandi, Tom and me at her pristine-white bungalow, reaching up to kiss us all. She wore a calf length brown plaid skirt, an earthy coloured jumper and a thick, dark green, handknitted cardigan. Her hair was wound in to a loose bun.

Her front room was stifling hot. A cheery fire sent out a rosy glow which was reflected back from the many porcelain figurines and vases that cluttered the mantelpiece, the sideboard and all along the windowsill. A ticking clock added a regular pulse to the occasional crackles from the fire. We three all squashed together on the two-seater sofa facing the fire.

If Sandi's mum had gone overboard in her welcome of Tom as a member of the family, her granny couldn't have appeared less bothered as she settled herself in to the rugs and cushions of her fireside chair. She closed her eyes for a moment behind the thick lenses of her glasses.

As she slowly opened her eyes a smile played around her lips and she held me transfixed with her gaze. 'You've started to see then?' she said. At least I think she said the words out loud. I certainly heard them clearly but Tom and Sandi paid no attention and continued talking about the weather, wondering if it was going to snow again today. I couldn't answer her. I stared into the fire, thinking about what she'd asked. Had I started to 'see'? She made it sound like I hadn't been looking before. I glanced back at her and she was nodding her head slightly.

Then she roused herself. 'Make some tea then, Sandi, and there's some tablet in the tin.' Tom spread himself along the sofa as Sandi went in to the kitchen.

'So this is our wee Tam,' she said.

'It's Tom. Tom Higgins,' I corrected but Tom nodded.

'I changed to Tom at school. It was bad enough Dad being a traveller without having a name that made me stick out as well.'

'No harm in that lad. We all have to live how we can. But you're amongst friends here.'

'I'm used to being Tom; that's what people know me as,' he said and shrugged.

Sandi came back in with the tray. She poured out four cups of dark brown tea and passed around the plate of syrupy-sweet tablet. We chatted idly for a while, mainly about Sandi's family members, most of whom I didn't know, and when we got up to leave I couldn't be sure of what had passed. Had Sandi's granny really tried to speak to me in some silent way? Or was it just my reaction to the heat in the room and the flickering firelight. Maybe I'd been the one to close my eyes and daydream? But at the front door she came close to me and I bent down towards her as she whispered, 'It's good to share what you know.' I nodded but I hadn't a clue what she was talking about.

She hugged Sandi and Tom then said, 'Come and see me again soon.' We set off together, arm in arm, stamping through the snow-covered lanes.

Tom left me at my back door and I went in alone. Frankie had eaten a late breakfast and had gone home, Dad was out walking, so it was just me and Mum. The house still needed more tidying but we left that and took our usual places in the kitchen, Mum perched on her high stool next to the stove, and me sitting at the small kitchen table where I usually get on with homework while Mum prepares tea.

'How was John?' she asked, sipping at a mug of coffee.

'Oh ... so, so.'

'Can't get used to being without you, heh?'

'I told him I didn't think there was a chance of us getting back together. He didn't take it very well. He seems to think things will be different when Tom leaves.'

'He might be right,' Mum said. She got up and started poking around in the fridge. 'Think it'll be scrambled eggs for tea,' she said. 'Is Tom coming this evening?'

It was amazing how soon Tom had become part of the normal conversations in our house. 'No, he's promised to play Scrabble with Mrs Fraser. And I'll be going to bed early. There's so much going on lately, I need a break.'

And I did too. I put on soft music and sank onto my bed. Staring at the ceiling, I considered the last few days. Was I 'seeing' things like Sandi's granny had said? Did she mean

I was some sort of psychic? Was I having premonitions? And who should I be sharing things with, Mum? Dad? Frankie? Tom? Was she suggesting that I should be talking to Tom about what was going on? About what I was supposedly seeing?

I mooched around my room for a while, changed my bed, put out my clothes for washing, flicked a duster over the top of my chest of drawers, sorted through old mags and generally kept my mind off the things that were bothering me. Then after a long soak in a warm, deep bath with lots of lavender oil, I went to bed and drifted in to a relaxed sleep.

I woke later, stiff with cold limbs. I huddled in to my downie but I couldn't get warm again. I knelt on my bed and peered out of the window. I shivered even more as I watched big white flakes glide down to join the already white covering on the ground. A full moon cruised through thick clouds. I pulled on a jumper and went down to the kitchen to fill a hot water bottle.

I couldn't resist the urge to open the back door and look out on the snowy world. Even though the moon was now hidden, I could see the snow piling up against the side of the house. Everything was eerily still and silent. I looked past the garden, beyond the orangey glow from the lights in the village and up to the hills. I wallowed in my memories of my recent walks with Tom. He belonged to this landscape. I couldn't imagine him fitting in anywhere else so well.

I glanced back at the garden, and there, in the middle of the lawn, I saw John and Tom fighting, snow being thrown up around them, and there were others, and someone on the ground. I was about to call out, run towards them but a sudden gust of wind swirled the snow lying at my feet and the image disappeared. The garden was empty, and just to prove it the moon came out of hiding and beamed a spotlight on the glittering snow.

I hurried back to my bed and cuddled the hottie. I was shaking from the cold and from what I'd seen. A few days ago, I would have thought I was having a bit of a dream. Even though I was standing out in the snow, it was the middle of the night. That's when you dream strange things. But since visiting Sandi's granny I was beginning to question everything. Was this a premonition? Were John and Tom going to fight? What would they be fighting about? I checked my phone. Both of them were still on my contact list.

Sixteen

I slept late the next morning and was woken by a message from Tom: 'Are you ever going to wake up? :)'

'Where are you?' I replied.

'Downstairs drinking coffee with your mum.'

I took a quick look out of my bedroom window. The garden was submerged in deep snow. The sky was bright blue and the sun was shining weakly through the trees.

Mum was showing Tom how to sprout beans when I made it downstairs. 'Just make sure you rinse them regularly,' she was saying, swirling water around a jar of newly germinated mung beans.

'When you've quite finished, Mrs. Mary Berry,' I said to Mum, 'Tom and I are needed outdoors.'

Tom picked up his jacket as I pulled him out the back door. The air was completely still. Piles of snow that were balanced unnaturally high on glossy leaves made tiny avalanches as the sun gave out a smidgen of warmth. Tom pointed out the comical tracks of birds in the deep crispy snow, and we decided the set of paw marks crossing the lawn had been made by a fox.

I was amazed that Tom didn't know how to make snow angels, so I demonstrated, getting snow in my hair and up my sleeves. We flopped on the doorstep, kicking snow at each other until our legs were completely white.

Then I received a message, 'gig tomorrow. Frankie is coming. Hope you can still make it. John.'

'What do you think?' I asked Tom. 'Should I go?'

'Why not?'

'Will you come too?'

'If you would like me to. I probably won't be much use but I'll do what I can. I finish about half five. What time do you need to leave?'

'Oh ... I forgot you're back to work tomorrow.'

'Yep. End of the hols today. Another three weeks of pipes and flow rates,' he said.

'Then you'll go back to college ... In Sunderland.'

'Look, Deidre, if this is going to be too difficult ...' He put an arm around me and I leant my head on his shoulder.

'No! I'm fine with it ... really.'

'Are you going to message back to John then?' Tom said gently. I nodded and wrote 'will be there at 6' to John.

'Have you any plans for today?' I asked as I put my phone back in my pocket. Tom unzipped his jacket and guided my hands under it to warm them.

'How about we have a walk then go out for lunch?'

'Mmm, lunch would be good ... but I'm starving now. I can't wait. I'll make us some cheese toasties and then we'll go for a walk.'

'I'll take you up to the site,' Tom said as we washed up.

'The bus has gone for today.'

'We can hitch a lift?'

Mum gave me a look but didn't say anything.

We lingered by the bus stop in the village. I'd convinced him that you didn't need to hitch in the conventional way around here. Anyone able to give you a lift will stop if they see you standing at the side of the road. Right enough, drivers of the first couple of cars gestured that they were turning in to the shop, or they were full up.

Then the white van with the distinctive 'Sound John' lettering on the side came around the bend. John pulled over, leaned across the passenger seats and wound down the window. 'I was only going for messages but where are you heading?' he asked.

'I'm taking Dee to the site ... it's only a couple of miles ... we could walk but the snow...' Tom said.

John opened the passenger door. 'Climb in then,' he said.

Tom let me slide in to the middle seat and jumped in beside me. I kept my knees firmly clamped together and my hands, prayer like, folded in my lap – avoiding contact with either boy.

'Back to work tomorrow then?' John asked Tom.

'Yeah. And yourself?'

'Yep.'

The snowplough had been out but the traffic was still moving quite slowly. It was even more difficult when we reached the turn in for the site as John had difficulty backing up in the snow. He gave us a wave as he pulled back onto the road but there was no smile. His face was set in an expressionless stare.

'He's a good guy,' Tom said. I didn't need Tom telling me. The whole world thinks that of John. We stomped along the snowy track up the hillside, neither of us saying any more. Above us icicles hung from exposed slabs of bare rock and beyond that was a steep ridge, scattered with granite boulders.

We reached a small, brick-built hut and Tom took out a key to let us in. It was dim inside until Tom hit a switch and a fluorescent strip light flickered on. It was even colder in the hut than outside and I blew through my gloves to warm my fingers. Below a small window, which gave a view up the hillside, there was a wooden bench with meters and dials fixed to it. Spades and a pickaxe were propped in a corner. Along another wall, a pin board held charts and notebooks marked by grubby fingers; a pencil dangled from a piece of string. A calendar still showed a skinny 'Miss December' wearing a tiny red bikini and a Santa hat. She clenched a piece of mistletoe between her teeth. Someone had coloured in a few of her front teeth with the black pencil.

Tom pointed through the window to show me the dam and the water pipes leading to the turbine.

'Not very fascinating or glamorous, I suppose,' I heard him say at the end of a long speech.

To be fair, I hadn't paid much attention. I certainly wouldn't have been able to answer questions on

Mastermind on flow rates and peak charts or whatever. But I was completely shaken when he said, 'It's all right. I won't come with you to the gig tomorrow. Then you can see John again. Sort out things with him.'

'What are you talking about?'

Tom took down the calendar and put it in the bin. 'I can see how things are. You deserve to be with someone better than me. Someone like—'

'Someone like John?' I finished for him.

Tom shrugged.

'How many times do I need to tell you? It's over with John. Completely.'

But I began to shake. Maybe John was just an excuse. Maybe Tom didn't like me now he'd got to know me. And, like Rhona had warned me not to, I'd let myself get in too deep. I'd fallen for Tom big time.

I couldn't stand around to hear his excuses. Before he could say any more I was out of the door, out of the gloomy artificial light in the hut to the glare of the sunlight reflecting off the snow.

I trudged further up the track. I could hear him behind me but I kept going.

'Wait, Dee. Let me explain. Please.'

I turned then. 'What? What do you need to explain?' I shouted.

He took a step towards me but I took a step back. He held out his hands towards me but I kept mine firmly in my pockets.

'I ... I want to ...' he said, his face twisting in anguish. Then he dropped his hands by his side. 'It's no use.'

I turned away and put my hands over my ears. He came up behind me; I could feel the warmth of his body.

I looked back at him and stared into his tortured face. 'Just say it then.' There would be no going back to John but if Tom wanted to finish things, I needed to hear it from him.

'I don't want to complicate things more ...' he started.

I gave a half laugh but there was a sob that wanted to follow it.

Then Tom took a deep breath and went on. 'Dee. I want to be with you. Be your boyfriend. I've got all the symptoms.'

'What?'

'Like you said ... about being in love.'

'You what?' Had I heard him correctly? Had he'd just said – being in love? 'For real?' I spluttered.

He nodded and closed the distance between us. I pressed my body close to his and, using the small amount of breath that was left in me I said, 'I feel the same.'

He looked into my eyes with disbelief. 'You're not kidding me?' I shook my head. 'You? But that's ... brilliant!'

He lifted me off the ground and rubbed the top of his head in to my belly. I felt his exuberance, his excitement. We started laughing and soon we'd tumbled over in the snow. Tom wasn't satisfied until we'd made a huge snow angel together, and when we got up to admire our efforts he drew on a tail and horns.

'That's you,' he said laughing. 'A devil disguised as

an angel.'

I caught my breath at what he'd said but Tom was back in the hut. He came out brandishing a large, plastic bin lid.

'Probably won't be very comfortable but we can give it a go.' He walked a bit further up the slope, took up position on the bin lid and dug in his heels. 'Come on,' he called.

I climbed behind him on the lid, wrapped my arms around his middle and peered over his shoulder.

'Ready?' He raised his feet and pushed off with his hands. After a faltering start, we hit the steep section and flew down. Trees loomed close, then rushed past. A whooshing ripped through my ears. We bumped and jolted over tussocks and outcrops, finally stopping near the road.

'Again?' he asked, and my grin was the only answer he needed.

On the third trip he made me sit in front of him. I was giddy with the closeness of his arms and legs surrounding me, his warm breath passing my cheeks in clouds. He kept his heels in the snow until I was ready, then we took off again but this time we veered off our original track and we were heading towards the trees. Tom leaned back, taking me with him and I glanced up at the sky. He dragged his feet in the snow and we slowed down slightly, then he rolled us off to one side and we tumbled down the hill. We pitched up in the lee of a large, spiky gorse bush. The bin lid lay abandoned a few metres above us.

'That was crazy,' I said at last.

Tom had landed sprawled across my legs. 'You're not hurt, are you? I was trying to save us. We were heading for the trees.'

'I'm fine.' I lay back in the snow, my arms and legs felt heavy, my breath came in quick gasps.

Tom pulled himself onto his knees and plucked a citrus-yellow flower from the gorse bush and held it out to me. 'There's a saying, "Only make love when the gorse is in bloom",' he said. Then, covered in confusion, he went on, 'I don't mean ... I wasn't thinking—'

'I know that saying,' I said quickly. 'I think in folklore 'making love' means falling in love, not ... you know ...' Now we were both embarrassed.

The sun was sinking behind the hills and my teeth started chattering. Tom helped me up and we brushed snow off each other. Back at the hut we returned the bin lid to its customary boring duties and Tom locked up.

It was starting to get dark when we reached the road and we walked quickly towards the village. Before long, a car pulled up to offer us a lift. This time it was tourists heading back to their chalet.

We'd finished tea and a call came through to my phone: Sandi.

'Can you come round?' she said without any hello or anything.

'I suppose so,' I said. 'Is something wrong?'

'Oh, no. Just be good to see you,' she said before ending the call.

Why didn't I believe her?

Mum and Dad were going out to a Bridge Club party so they gave us a lift to Sandi's.

'Great. Hi Tom,' Sandi said, pushing us in to the living room and putting on her coat. 'Mum has gone with Dad to the Bridge and she made me promise I'd stay in. She still thinks I'm gonna faint or something,' she said, pointing to her head which had lost its bandage. 'But I need to go out – just for a wee while. She probably won't phone but if she does, you can cover for me. Say I'm in the loo or something and message me. I won't be long.' There was a beeping from a car outside.

'I don't think this is a good idea ...' I started but Sandi was already out the door.

Tom and I sat on the sofa and flicked through the TV channels.

'I feel like a negligent babysitter who's let the baby escape,' I said. I went through to the kitchen and put the kettle on to boil, thinking I'd make a cup of tea.

Tom followed me, looking awkward. 'I still feel bad about what happened at the party here.'

'It's okay,' I said.

'How could I have been such a fool?' he went on.

'I'm repeatedly reminded that it's a part of growing up.'

He put his arms around me and kissed the top of my head.

'You didn't really do anything. Not when you realised the truth.' I hesitated, and then asked him, 'Will you do something for me?'

'Of course. Anything.'

I took his hand and led him to the stairs.

'What are you doing?' he asked.

'I think they call it laying ghosts.'

We reached the top of the stairs and I pulled him towards me to kiss him. He kissed me back, warmly. Then I manoeuvred him towards the old playroom. The door was slightly open and I could see the window with the half-closed blind.

Still locked in each other's arms we entered the room, taking stumbling steps through the boxes. He looked at me questioningly and then relaxed as he understood.

We stood close to each other, looking into each other's eyes. The orange glow from the streetlight fell on the serious line of his mouth. There was no thud of music below but I could hear my heart beating with my quickening pulse.

'I should never have left you that night. I should have stayed at the party, made sure you were safe,' he whispered.

'Frankie looks out for me. And you did try to phone me.'

'How pathetic is that? And then I ran off. If you hadn't come to find me ... I don't deserve you.' He cupped my face in his hands.

The growl of a car approaching made us part and I looked out of the window, half fearing the return of Sandi's parents. What I saw was possibly worse. Sandi was getting out of the car and it looked like Matt sitting in the driving seat. We were heading downstairs as she came in.

'Was that Matt in the car?' I asked.

'He was doing me a wee favour,' Sandi said. She waved cans of cider at us. 'Thanks guys. You've no idea how awful it is being cooped up. You two had a nice time?' she added, nodding towards the stairs.

Tom and I replied at the same time. 'Well, apart from wondering what on earth you are up to, we're okay,' I said, while Tom said: 'Very.'

Sandi laughed at us. 'Don't mind me,' she called, carrying her cans through to the front room. 'I'm gonna watch another movie.'

Tom made some tea for us and we joined her.

We walked back to my house, and even though Mum and Dad were still out we found our sheltered spot by the back door to say goodbye.

'Thanks for today,' Tom said.

'I can't believe I won't be able to see you so much now. It seems so unfair ... after today.'

'It'll be the weekend soon.'

'Yeah, then after that I'll be back at school, and straight in to exams and Mum and Dad will keep me chained to revising.'

'We'll find time for each other. And we can make it the best time.'

'But you'll be gone so soon.'

'Like you said, heh? We can take it one day at a time.'

Seventeen

'I'm being asked some awkward questions about the state of the bin lid!' Tom's message read next morning.

'Tell them you had to use it to beat off all the girls xx' I replied.

I had a mountain of homework to do and I tried to get on with it but my mind kept drifting back to Tom and our time in the snow, and Tom and our time in the croft, and Tom and his soft lips.

So, when he called by after work, I'd hardly touched the piles of textbooks and jotters scattered around.

We walked down to Le Club. John's van was in the car park and I could hear Alec's voice testing a mic, 'One, two ... one, two.' I ran on ahead and in through the backstage door. Five or six lads were piling out, pulling on jackets, talking about the gig and complimenting John's engineering skills and his quick work.

'What's happening?' I shouted at John. He was standing at his mixing desk. Frankie and Sandi were tidying cables at the front of the stage.

'Dee! Sorry, I thought you weren't coming. Sandi asked if I could train her up if you ... aren't so interested anymore.'

'I messaged you ... said I'd be here for six.'

'Sorry, I didn't get that. The band from Glasgow needed an early sound check. They're heading to dinner now.'

'Hey John, have you got another mic for when Slim does backing vocals?' a lad from the stage spoke through his mic.

'Sorry, Dee, I'll have to get on,' John said. Then he called out, 'Frankie, can you show Sandi where the 58s are and set one up for Slim.' John looked back at me. I was still rooted to the spot. Then he glanced over to Tom who was standing in the shadows at the side of the stage. 'Hope you can both stay for the gig though.'

That was me dismissed then.

I joined Tom and checked my phone. Right enough, the message to John hadn't been delivered. I hadn't noticed.

'Want a coffee?' Tom asked.

'Yes please.'

We went through to the bar. The band from Glasgow was sitting at a table by the window, still laughing and joking. And in the midst of them were Amy, Rhona and Matt.

I wasn't good company. If I'd been with Mum, she would have told me to stop sulking. But Tom kept quiet. He started flicking a beermat, making it spin in the air then catching it. It was beginning to annoy me but then he slid one towards me and gave a big grin. I copied his actions and after a few misses, with the beermat ending on the floor, I soon had the beermat twisting in mid-air before catching it myself.

'Simple things please simple minds.' Matt wasn't looking at us but I knew his comment was intended for us to overhear. Amy guffawed, sounding like a braying donkey, and wound her red, silky shirted arm around Matt's neck.

'Do you want to go home?' Tom slid his warm hand on my lap.

'I'm not going to let those eejits think they've driven me away.'

'But you don't look very happy.'

'Besides,' I continued, 'I'd like to see the gig and there won't be time to get home and back again,' I said and drained my mug of coffee.

'How about a game of pool then?'

I nodded and we went through to the pool room. I'm actually not bad and I won the first game. After a couple of games Rhona appeared at the door and beckoned me.

'I'll be back in a mo,' I said to Tom and then I followed Rhona into Le Ladies.

'You'll have to help with Amy,' Rhona said grabbing my hands.

'And in what universe would I be likely to do that?'

'Come on, Dee. She's obsessed with Matt. She's planning to stay with him tonight. She wants me to cover for her. We've got to make her see reason.'

'She'd not take any notice of what I say anyway.'

'He's just using her, I'm sure. You can tell by how he looks at her when she can't see him.'

'Well, can't you go with her? Stop her doing anything stupid.'

'I thought if we all go that might help. I wonder if we could get a lift. Will your parents be okay with that?'

'Rhona! I'm not going to stay at Matt's house. You know what he's like. You'll have to get Amy home somehow. Frankie and Sandi will be through soon, they'll have better ideas than me.'

With that I went back to the pool room.

'Rhona's in a right stew ...' I started but then I saw Matt; he was squaring up to Tom. But worse was the stunned look on Tom's face.

Matt turned to glance at me. 'You might not be so popular with the ladies when they find out,' he said to Tom before he turned to go back to the bar.

'It's okay,' Tom said, putting a protecting arm around me.

'What's that creep up to?'

'Not now ... I tell you later.'

'You look like you've seen a ghost.'

'It's okay. It'll be fine.' But he looked done in.

'He hasn't hurt you, has he?'

'No. It's nothing like that ... Come on. Can we get a sandwich or something?'

We went back in to the bar. The party at the window table was breaking up. The band's dinner had arrived and Rhona, Amy and Matt were heading to the venue. They took no notice of Tom and me.

Alec was singing with the local band, Kneejerk, who were on first and I had time to catch up with Frankie.

'Things still good between you and Alec then?'

'Better than good. Absolutely dead brilliant!'

During the break, Frankie and I went outside to cool down while Tom fetched us Cokes from the bar. The snow had stopped falling but the car park was still covered in a thick white layer. Only a few cars had made it in, most people preferring to park on the road. I recognised one as Matt's.

The path from the door was icy and folk hung around the porch where a dim light cast elongated shadows: some were smoking, some passing around cans of coke, doubtless with vodka added. Sandi was with a group of girls from town and I was surprised to see her sharing a joint with them.

'You okay with Tom?' Frankie asked.

'Better than okay.'

'When's he going back to Sunderland?'

'Why does everyone ask me that?'

'Sorry. You know I don't want to see you get hurt.'

'He went to work today. I missed him like hell.'

Frankie hugged me.

'You still don't like him, do you?' I said.

'Are you sure you don't like him just because he's a bit different?'

I nodded. 'I do like that he's not the same as everyone from round here. Life is definitely more fun when he's about.' Frankie scowled. 'But it's more than that. He likes me for who I am. He seems to need me somehow. I can't explain.'

She shrugged. 'He always seems self-reliant to me.'

'I think that's because he can fend for himself. But he's unsure about so many other things.'

Frankie gazed at the dark sky.

'You will be nice to him ... for me,' I said.

'So long as he doesn't hurt you,' she said, giving me a hug.

Tom came back from the bar balancing three Cokes on top of each other. Frankie took hers, gave a 'cheers' to Tom, sipped from her can and wandered back indoors.

'She's going to need a lot of convincing, isn't she?'

'What?'

'I know she thinks I'm not good enough for you. I suppose John is a hard act to follow. I'll have to prove my worth.'

'You don't have to prove anything. You're as good as any of them.'

He didn't answer. And I remembered the look on his face when he was with Matt in the pool room.

Sandi was nowhere to be seen at the end of the gig, so Frankie, John and I went in to our routine to pack away. John gave me a thankful smile. Tom hovered. He couldn't help much but he shouldered bags out to the van when he could. Between us, we loaded up the van, slipping and sliding on the icy path.

Matt and a couple of his goons were hanging around in the carpark. They threw a few snowballs at us and laughed raucously when they found their target.

'You waiting for something?' John called over to them.

'Don't believe it's any of your business if we are,' Matt chirped. The goons laughed even more. Matt lolled against his car swigging beer from a bottle.

Then Rhona and Amy came out from the porch. Rhona's face was bright red. She'd either been crying or was very cross.

'You ready babe?' Matt called to Amy. Then I knew what the matter with Rhona was.

'I've told her I won't cover for her but she says she doesn't care. Says she sixteen, she can do what she likes,' Rhona said to me.

John overheard. 'She not going off with that creep, is she?'

'She staying the night with him,' Rhona whimpered.

'Over my dead body!' John was across the car park in no time. All the laughing and chatter stopped dead.

John knocked the beer from Matt's hand.

'You want to watch it, mate,' Matt growled.

'Get this – mate. For one, if you try and drive this vehicle, I'll be calling the police, and two, you go anywhere near Amy and I'll flatten you.'

'No skin off my nose,' Matt shrugged, 'I'm not planning on driving home yet. I need a few more beers.' The goons laughed again. 'And you're welcome to the slut.'

John's right fist made a squelch as it hit Matt full in the face. Amy screamed.

Matt's goons fell on John, planting punches anywhere

they could.

I felt Tom's jacket fall across my shoulders and with a few strides Tom was in the middle of the fight, helping John. Tom aimed a punch in Matt's stomach and Matt doubled over before falling to the ground. Finally, first one, then the other goons ran off towards the village. Matt lay sprawled out in the snow. Tom was on his knees, his head tipped back.

John stumbled towards us, fingering a swollen lip. Amy perched on the wall with her head in her hands, crying and moaning, yet stealing glances towards John as he approached.

But my eyes were fixed on Tom as he struggled to stand. Matt lifted his head. The dim light from the porch reflected on something in his hand. In a moment, Matt jumped up, pushed Tom over, sprinted to his car and drove out of the car park at speed, his tyres skidding on the icy tarmac.

Tom staggered to his feet. I watched his hand move to a place on his white shirt where a dark stain was spreading. I rushed towards him but before I could reach him, he glanced at me then ran out of the carpark, clutching his side.

John was at my side and held on to my arm as I tried to follow Tom. 'Squeeze in the van with Amy and Rhona. I'll take you all home,' he said.

'What about Tom?' I yelled. 'He's hurt.'

'We'll pick him up. Just get in.'

'No!' I screeched. John was pulling me towards the van. 'Find Tom.' John nodded and jumped in his van. He pulled out of the carpark heading in the direction Tom had taken.

I leaned against the low wall. 'I saw it. I saw it!'

Frankie sat next to me. 'What?'

'I saw the fight.'

'We all saw it, Dee. Matt started it – again.'

'No. You don't understand ... a couple of nights ago. I saw the fight. Tom and John were fighting; there was someone on the ground. And now Tom is hurt.'

Alec came out to the porch and Frankie ran up to him. I could tell they were discussing me. Alec looked across at me and although he was frowning, he was nodding his head.

Frankie came back and squatted in front of me. 'Dee, look at me. Alec will take you home. The band will wait until he gets back. You need to get home.'

'I can't. I've got to wait for Tom. He's hurt.' I ran my hands over my shoulders. 'He's not even got a jacket.'

'But Dee. He ran off.'

'Not from me.'

Frankie didn't answer straight away. 'John will find Tom and take him home. Tom will call you when he's ready, I'm sure.'

'Stop talking to me like I'm a five-year-old.'

'Well stop acting like one.'

'You just don't like Tom.'

'Can you blame me? Look at the state of you.'

'Frankie, don't make me have to choose.'

'What!' she exploded, 'Between me and him. It's come to that has it?' And she stormed off.

Alec led me to where the band's van was parked at the stage door and opened the passenger door. I pushed my arms in to Tom's jacket, zipped it up and climbed in the van.

Back at home, I called to Mum to let her know I was in but I didn't want to talk. I lay on my bed, still fully clothed. All I could think about was Tom. Was he badly hurt? Had John found him? But I couldn't bring myself to call or message Tom. Frankie was right. He had run off – had it been to get away from me? Had Tom done something wrong? Matt had said something to Tom in the pool room that had changed everything.

Eighteen

I was extra careful not to make any sound as I let myself out of the back door. I'd put on a woolly hat and gloves and I kept on Tom's jacket but I wasn't going to get out my wellies; my trainers would have to do.

Nothing was moving in the night. It was as if the ice had frozen everything in to place. The banks of snow crunched when I crossed them to get to the gritted road. I ran most of the way.

There were no lights on at Mrs Fraser's, no signs of life at all. Skirting the house, I looked up at Tom's bedroom window. I climbed on the bin and pulled up against the lean-to. I could probably get on the sloping roof of the lean-to and reach Tom's window but it was closed and I was sure I'd make a terrible racket.

I went to the front again and leaned against the porch door, wishing I was small enough to use the cat flap. I almost resorted to knocking on the door. Then I tried the handle. It turned effortlessly in my hand and the door opened. A black cat appeared from the shadows, ran past me and in to the porch.

It took a while for my eyes to get used to the darkness indoors after the snow-bright outside. I hugged the wall as I climbed the stairs. The door to Tom's room was slightly ajar. It gave a faint creak as I opened it gently.

The curtains at the small window overlooking the back yard were still open. I could make out the outline of the desk and chair and the bed against the wall. I patted the covers on the bed. He wasn't there.

I pushed the door closed again and stretched out on top of the bed. I didn't have a plan. I couldn't rehearse what I wanted to say to him. I just needed to know he was safe – and I wanted him to know I loved him, no matter what.

I don't know how long I lay like that, eyes wide open, ears strained for any minute sound but then I heard someone outside. Someone opened the porch door who knew they didn't need a key; there were footsteps on the stairs from someone who knew how to keep quiet. A trembling hand opened the bedroom door.

'Tom,' I whispered.

'What the ...'

Tom sidestepped around the bed and switched on his bedside lamp. We stared at each other for ages, neither of us speaking. He looked dreadful. His face was white; his whole body trembled. The stain on his shirt was drying a dark brown. Still clutching his side, he opened the wardrobe and took out his rucksack. Putting a finger to his lips he beckoned me to follow him.

Down in the kitchen he closed the door and turned on a couple of lamps. Tom picked up the kettle but I took it off him and filled it.

'Tea?'

He nodded.

I found the teapot and mugs and made myself busy whilst stealing glances at Tom. He took a green box out of the rucksack, stripped off his shirt and held it against his side. His hand was trembling as he fought with the catch on the first aid box. I took it from him and opened it. It was well stocked and I took out sterile wipes and an assortment of dressings.

He peeled away his shirt and we inspected the wound together. I soaked a clean tea towel in warm water and wiped away the blood that had run down his side.

The gash was about three or four centimetres long and quite deep at one end where the knife had sliced through his skin. The edges were swollen and a livid red. Blood was still oozing out.

'I think this needs stitches,' I said. But he shook his head and sorted through the dressings, choosing one that would cover the wound.

By the time we had the wound relatively clean his trembles had subsided to deep shivers.

'I'm going to get a jumper from upstairs,' he said.

When he came down again I'd made the tea and found some cake.

I needed to tell him, although I knew it would sound odd. 'I saw the fight,' I whispered.

Tom struggled in to his jumper and gave a 'uh huh'.

'It was before it happened. It was a bit like a dream but I wasn't asleep.' I was amazed that this was the first time I'd told Tom anything about the unusual things that were happening to me. 'You don't think I'm weird, do you?'

Tom smiled for the first time since he'd come in. He shook his head and took hold of my hand. 'Ssh ... we'll talk tomorrow.' His fingers were still icy cold. He switched off the lamps in the kitchen and led me back upstairs.

Tom pulled off the downie and lay gingerly on the bed, his back towards the wall. I took off his jacked, snuggled in next to him and pulled the downie over us.

We moulded our bodies together. Tom wrapped his arms around my tummy and breathed deeply in to my hair. Soon the shared warmth of our bodies stilled Tom's shivers.

I woke feeling Tom's fingers stroking my hair. 'We'd better get you back before you're missed,' he whispered.

I turned to him and lightly kissed his lips. 'You stay here. I can get back myself.'

He laughed quietly and pulled himself up. He picked up his jacket to put it on, then remembered I'd been wearing it and put it on me again.

'Message me as soon as you get back,' I made him promise when we got near my back door.

'And I'll call by after work if that's okay with you?'

'You're going to work! But what about your side.'

'If it's still bleeding in the morning, I'll let nurse Fraser have a look.'

The sounds when I woke next morning were all wrong. I

could hear water running. Outside? And there were none of the usual morning sounds like the radio chunnering away, or dishes being washed, or Mum whistling Beatles songs.

I decided to investigate the running water first and peered out the window. A huge slab of snow slid past, making a roar like thunder on the roof. The crisp white snow on the window ledge had turned a translucent grey.

Despite the thaw outside, I shivered. I pulled on a hoody over my jammies and wandered downstairs. There was no one about. I found a note on the kitchen table. 'Taken Dad to town.'

I filled the kettle for tea and remembered doing the same thing just a few hours earlier at Mrs Fraser's. I checked the kitchen clock; Tom would be on site, that's if he hadn't collapsed with blood loss or something.

I took my tea and a few digestives up to bed and snuggled down again. But I was restless. I couldn't get over having a vision of the fight in the snow. I got up and peered into my mirror. Was I some sort of psychic? My hair looked the same mousy brown, my nose still podgy and my lips too large. My eyes hadn't turned a witchy green. I tried closing them and emptying my mind. Would my psychic consciousness drift up and show me more visions? I didn't believe it would.

I dragged my school bag onto my bed and took out some revision notes but harsh memories of what had happened outside Le Club blurred the words. Then I heard Mum's car pull up outside. Dr Jekyll and Mr Hyde would have to wait.

'Where's Dad?'

Mum dropped in her chair in the living room. 'Phone call in the middle of the night. Nine o'clock in India, four o'clock here. I ended up taking him to the airport.'

'He's gone?'

'There's some trouble with the railway. He's going to try and get back in a couple of weeks.' She tried to stifle a yawn.

'You know that never happens. He's always gone for months. I don't know why you put up with it.'

'And what am I supposed to do? We can't traipse around the world with him.'

I don't know why I hadn't realised before. 'That's what you'd do if it wasn't for me, isn't it? You'd be able to go with him. You have to stay here because of me.'

Mum gave me a funny look. 'You need to be at school somewhere. It's better here than a series of International Schools.'

She looked dreadful, her eyes bleary and her hair lank against her face. I knew I shouldn't keep on at her. 'Had you considered that?'

She opened her eyes wide and straightened her head. 'We considered lots of things before you were born. I hope you think we made the right decision.'

I went on, knowing I shouldn't. 'And you don't regret it?'

Mum jumped up and hugged me. 'Don't ever think that. I love living here with you ... But I do miss your dad.'

'Tea,' I said, pushing her back in her chair, 'and

Smarties. That's what we need.' I took a tube from Mum's secret hiding place.

I sent Mum back to bed and made fussing her my project for the day. A text came in later from Dad: 'Sorry didn't see you to say goodbye. I'll get back soon. Keep safe. Love you, Dad xx'

I made a huge spag bog for tea and Tom helped eat it when he came after work. I wanted to ask him about his wound but I couldn't with Mum there. Tom was fed up that Dad had left so unexpectedly too. They'd planned for Dad to visit the site at the weekend.

Mum said she needed to read the paper for half an hour after tea and could Tom and I wash up. She gave us a barely concealed wink and I blushed as I realised it was her plan to give us time alone.

'So, is it okay?' I whispered, pointing at his stomach.

He gave a shrug and a nod at the same time. 'I think so.' Then he leaned back against the sink, his legs wide apart, and pulled me towards him. 'I wish I hadn't eaten so much,' he said as he nibbled at my ear.

'Stop being so cheesy.'

But he kissed my neck and soon we were locked together, without any care for the dishes.

'It's Saturday tomorrow. No work,' Tom said as he was leaving later that evening.

'Shall we go up to the croft? We can take some lunch.'

He seemed to think about it for a while then said, 'Okay.'

I scanned his face. 'There's something you're not

telling me?'

He gave a single nod. 'Lots.'

Nineteen

We left the village and walked along the shore. The tide was drifting out, exposing rocks and dragging air through tight crevices like an old lady sucking her teeth. A constant, salty wind stung my cheeks. Circling gulls, cackling like raucous day trippers, emphasised our silence as we tramped along. We tucked in to our hidden cove and sheltered among the rhododendrons using a knotty ledge of exposed roots for a seat.

Tom plucked the fronds off a nearby fern. 'I've been thinking ... I don't think we should come out like this.'

'What's the matter? Why do say things like that?'

'It's not safe.'

'Why not?'

He shook his head.

'You say you want to be with me. Well then, why don't you trust me. Tell me what's bothering you.' Even though I felt frustrated with him, his eyes looked so sad. 'Please,' I begged. 'Tell me.'

He nodded. 'All right ... It's Matt. He's not going to stop.'

I hadn't forgotten the look on Tom's face in the pool room. 'He knows something about you?'

Tom looked resigned. 'He knows things about Mam's family that even I didn't know. Things best kept secret. But I'll tell you what I know ... It's only fair. Then you can choose if you still want to know me.'

He took out the folded paper showing his family tree that he kept in his pocket. We both looked at it in the shadows. Tom had made more entries after speaking to Sandi and her mum.

'It's a long story ... and it started around here, on the croft, when Mam's grandparents stayed here. I told you Mam's grandfather was a strict man, and his only daughter—'

'Your grandmother. And she was related to Sandi's mum?'

'That's her. She was seeing this chap and they weren't very careful and she got pregnant.'

'I remember that bit too. That was with your mam.'

'Well. I think Mam's grandfather knew who the father was really but he made up a story that she'd been raped by one of the travellers staying near the village.'

'That's awful,' I said.

'It gets worse. There was talk of the traveller putting a curse on the family. Then when her grandfather died, Mam and her grandmother had to leave the croft. But none of the relatives nearby could help very much. They had enough troubles of their own I expect.'

'So what did they do?'

'Mam's grandmother had moved from the North

East of England when she got married, so she took Mam back to be near her family there. That's where later on Mam met my dad.

'And your great-granny helped them set up in a flat?'

'Well it was her relatives, yeah. I knew most of that from Dad but Matt told me that the traveller who was implicated was his grandfather. And now Matt wants revenge.'

I'd got a bit lost following the generations but I said, 'So one of your ancient relatives blamed one of Matt's ancient relatives for something he didn't do and now Matt's out to settle the score.'

'That's about it. Although it's not that ancient really. Matt's family have since settled in town but they still bear the scar of that injustice.'

'You're not defending him, I hope.'

'Not defending him, no – he doesn't need to resort to violence. But I understand that he feels he has to try and set the record straight ... clear his grandfather's name. Matt won't stop until he's regained his family's honour.'

'He's a sadistic slimeball.'

'Yeah, he's that too.'

We sat in silence again for a while but this time it felt more like we were sharing each other's stories.

'I don't think I want to go up to the croft,' I said.

'No. I'll go—'

'Don't be stupid. Let's go home,' I said, heading back to the shore. 'This wind is enough to blow the sense out of anyone's brain.'

Back at home, Mum hardly looked up as we went in. She was fetching tins of paint out of the utility room. 'Frankie called. Said she couldn't get you on your mobile,' she said, prising the lid off a tin of white emulsion.

I tapped my pocket. 'I must have left it upstairs.'

There was a message from her, 'we need to talk'

Tom took a fleecy tartan blanket from my bed and spread it on the floor. We emptied the food onto it. Through the night, I'd had romantic notions of eating our lunch sitting together cosy in the croft, before a roaring fire. But, in a way, this was better; this was real.

'Plan B?'

Tom nodded approval. I put on the music while he poured tea out of the flask.

We sat cross legged, facing each other, unwrapping squashed sandwiches and crumbly cake.

There was a thundering of feet on the stairs, then a soft tapping on my door. Frankie poked her head in before I could get up.

'Only me. Your mum said to come up.' She was smiling.

Tom got up and picked up his jacket.

'Don't leave because of me. I'm glad you're here,' Frankie said. That got me worried but she was still smiling.

So we all settled on the floor around the assorted bits of food. I've done less bizarre things on a Saturday afternoon.

'Right. Which of you two love birds is going to tell me what's going on?'

Tom and I stared at each other. But Frankie wasn't going to shift until she'd heard the truth.

'Should I ...?' I asked Tom. He nodded and so I told her everything. She listened without interrupting as I recounted all about Tom's family history and about how Matt wanted revenge.

Frankie had eaten some sandwiches while I talked and she'd left the crusts in a neat pile. 'So, Matt knew about you and Sandi being cousins?' she asked.

'He must have done,' Tom said.

'The revolting texts,' I said, 'They were from Matt.'

'Undoubtedly,' Frankie concluded. 'I can understand why Tom doesn't want to drag you in to all this. Matt is pure evil. And ... I can see you're completely crazy about each other.'

'I know you don't approve,' I said.

'Who am I to approve or disapprove?'

'Only my best friend.'

'No,' she said laughing, 'what with you seeing visions and Tom always running off, you'll make a wonderful couple.'

Tom gave a quick glance towards me, then tried to hide it.

'You haven't told him, have you?' Frankie said.

'Dee mentioned something. I just haven't got the whole account yet,' he said reaching out to take my hand. 'I suppose I've monopolised the whole storytelling bit.'

'I've got to get cat food from the shop. That'll give you two some time to get to know each other a bit better,' she said glaring at me. 'And then we're going to Sandi's. I reckon she should know some of this at least.'

'No wonder Frankie didn't want me near you. Your life has been turned upside down since I came on the scene.' I hadn't held back on telling him all the things that were bothering me.

'But I still can't explain anything. Do you believe in premonitions? Do you think I'm telepathic or something? If it was just the phone thing I'd be happy to accept it was a coincidence; I'd laugh it off after a while. But hearing Sandi's granny in my head, and seeing you and John fighting in the snow before it happened ... Do you think I was cursed in some way? Do you believe in curses?'

'Calm down,' he said, pulling me on to the bed and holding me. 'No, I don't believe in them,' he said gently. 'I suppose, in a way, I'm living proof that I don't.'

'Even with all that bad luck in your family ... and your mam—'

'She had breast cancer. They found it late. She didn't get cured.'

'You don't believe the curse had anything to do with it?'

'What about the good luck of Mam being taken to Sunderland and meeting Dad. They were very happy and very much in love. And if our family being cursed brought me back here, to meet you ... well then, I'm glad of it.'

'So I'm not cursed then?'

'When have you ever done anything to make anyone even want to try such a thing?' he said. 'But I know what you mean about Sandi's granny. I felt odd near her too.

Sort of like she was trying to read my mind. Maybe she couldn't get through to me as clearly as to you.'

'Oh, I'm so glad!'

'What? Why?'

'Well, if you didn't think there was any truth in the whole telepathy thing, then I would have to be losing the plot.'

'Meet me at bakery. I'm still hungry' came in a message from Frankie.

We tidied up my room then Tom threw his rucksack over his shoulder. I could tell his side was still painful and I made him show me the wound. He'd put on fresh dressings but the flesh around the cut was swollen and still weeping pus.

'It's mending,' he said.

'I hate Matt.'

'Ssh. Don't talk of hate.'

I stroked the bruise on his face from the earlier fight. 'Let's go and meet Frankie then.'

The bakery was busy and Frankie was at the front of the queue when we joined her. John's mum held open a white cardboard box and Frankie was choosing a selection of cakes and pastries to fill it. She pointed at a chocolate éclair, looked at me, and I nodded.

'Can't chat now. Come and see me later,' John's mum said and she blew us kisses as we left her sweet-smelling shop.

Our wellies left deep holes in the gritty slush as we squelched our way up Sandi's drive.

Loud rock music was coming from Sandi's room.

There didn't appear to be anyone home downstairs so we headed up the stairs. Frankie bounded ahead of us and opened the door to Sandi's room. 'Oh sorry,' she said and quickly shut the door again.

This time she knocked heavily and waited until the music stopped and Sandi came to the door.

'Great. Come in,' Sandi said.

We all piled into her tiny bedroom. John was sitting on the edge of the bed, his hands clasped tight on his knees.

'Cakes anyone,' Frankie said, trying to hide her embarrassment.

We all found somewhere to perch, and Frankie proceeded to tell Sandi and John about Matt and his vendetta, with explanations from Tom when she got things a bit wrong.

Then Sandi, Frankie and John all started talking at once, only half listening to each other. They all agreed that Matt needed putting a stop to. Their plan, if it could be called that, amounted to setting Tom up as bait with the gang waiting in the wings to pounce on Matt when he started a fight.

Anger rose up in me, tightening my chest. 'No,' I shouted. 'This isn't some kind of kid's adventure. Tom has suffered enough at the hands of that idiot. Matt's not going to have the chance to pull a knife on him again.'

'What! Matt has a knife?' Frankie exploded.

I nodded and with my persuasion Tom pulled up his jumper to show the dressing on his side.

Frankie looked fearsome. 'That boy has gone too far.

Who does he think he is causing fights all over the place and stabbing our friends?'

'Let's think about this rationally,' John said.

'What does Matt want, do you think?' Sandi asked.

'I suppose he wants to humiliate me and cause me severe damage in the process,' Tom said.

'Do you think Alec has any influence over him?' I asked Frankie.

'I'm not sure. I'll talk to him if you want. I'm seeing him tonight.'

'Surely the more people on our side the better,' Sandi said.

We all nodded.

'I think, until we've made some sort of plan to deal with Matt, you should keep your head down, Tom,' John said. 'And the same for you, Dee, stay at home,' he added.

I wanted to argue, say that I wasn't going to be held prisoner in my own house by some bully boy but how could I with Tom at risk.

We were a despondent crew eating our fancy cakes and eventually Frankie, Tom and I got up to go.

As we were leaving, John pulled me to one side. 'It wasn't what it looked like when you came in. Sandi's having trouble with her speaker. She asked me to have a look at it.'

'Sounds like you've fixed it then.'

'I can't stand not going out. We could be careful – keep away from where Matt hangs out,' I said when Tom walked me back home.

'Or when.'

'What do you mean?'

'I don't think he'll be sitting up all night watching for me.'

'We could go out at night?'

'Not a good idea, I know.'

'It's the best,' I said.

'It's not fair on your mum.'

'She won't know I'm gone. Nothing's going to happen.'

'Well, okay. I'll be out the back later. Don't worry if you change your mind. I'll message you.'

I was greedy to see him. I was selfish. I put my own thoughts of pleasure before our safety, before Mum's trust in me.

We could have stayed near the house. We could have kept to the village but we set off walking. Without saying anything about where we were heading, we climbed through the remains of the snow, uphill to the white rock.

I used my windup torch from time to time through the trees but the moon was a shiny coin high in the sky and cast enough light to guide us for most of the way.

We leaned against the rock, side by side.

'That first day I met you here. Your face was wet.'

Tom nodded.

'Had you been crying?' I asked.

'I was telling Mam things.'

'Telling her? How?'

'Well. She's here; in every blade of grass, every frond

of fern, and every flower in the spring.' He took hold of my hand, his fingers interlaced with mine. 'This is where me and Dad scattered her ashes.'

I stood rigid; scared to move my feet in case I crushed the grass that was growing with bits of Tom's mam in it.

'This spot was special to her then?'

'Mmm. She even had a name for the rock. Stumpy, or something like that. She told me lots of stories, all about the people who used to live here.'

I had a sudden flash of the vision I'd seen of Tom walking amongst the ghostly figures on the hillside. 'Sandi's granny,' I said.

'What?'

'We need to see Sandi's granny.'

'Why?'

'I don't know. It just came in to my head. We'll go and see her tomorrow. Well, later today. Mum will take us.'

'Was it only a feeling?'

'Yes. But not one I want to ignore.'

Twenty

Mum was a bit put out when I asked her to pick Tom up and take us to Sandi's granny's on Sunday afternoon but she didn't ask any questions. She dropped us at the lane end and we walked up to the house.

'I'm a bit scared,' I said.

Tom took a step ahead and knocked on the door. Sandi's granny must have been right behind it, because it opened immediately.

'There we are now. Come away in,' she said.

The room was as hot as last time we called, the fire was still roaring away in the grate. This time there was a table set under the window. A white cloth with crocheted edges covered the table, four china cups and saucers and a plate of sandwiches covered with cling film were neatly laid out. A tiny glass vase with snow drops graced the centre of the table.

'I'm sorry. Are we interrupting?' I said.

'Not at all. Come away in and sit down.' Tom and I sat on the sofa facing the fire.

'I hope you don't mind me asking, but did you know

my mam?' Tom asked with his usual lack of preamble when Sandi's granny had settled herself in her fireside chair.

'I did indeed. I used to mind her when she was a wee bairn. She was so adventurous when she started to walk; it was hard keeping up with her. My sister-in-law, Marie, your Mam's grandmother that is, was run ragged by her, so I would take her for a while to let Marie have a rest. She had a favourite place she always headed to.'

'A white rock?' Tom said.

Sandi's granny made a strange noise in her throat, which I supposed was a laugh. 'That's the place. She had some funny name for it.'

Tom pulled out the family tree and handed it to Sandi's granny. 'So, Mam's grandfather was—'

'My elder brother – that's right – the one that caused all the trouble. Course he's dead now and can't make amends. Your grandmother wanted to marry Tam. But my brother wouldn't allow it. He didn't think a man who could get a girl in the family way before they were married was worth having as a husband.'

'Tam?' Tom repeated in a small voice.

'Aye, your mother wasn't ashamed to own her father, although she never met him of course. She named you for him. His full name is Robert Thomas Cameron but he's known to everyone as Big Tam.'

'So, he's still alive?'

'Of course. Hale and hearty; lives not too far out of the village.'

'He knows about me?'

'Been waiting to meet you these last seventeen years.'

'He wants to meet me?' Tom's voice gave away his emotions.

'Not unless it's what you want,' Sandi's granny said, quietly.

'It is.' The look of shock that had taken hold of Tom's face as he listened to the news was replaced by a small smile. 'It is what I want.'

'Well, pass me that phone then.'

Tom stretched behind him to pick up the handset and passed it to her. He looked as if he was in a dream.

Sandi's granny tapped in a few numbers and spoke in to the phone, 'Aye he's here, like I said ... Of course he does ... That's good ... Cheerie.'

She passed the handset back to Tom and he replaced it.

We all sat in silence for a few moments then she said, 'I'll brew the tea then,' and went in to the kitchen.

Tom still didn't say a word but he gazed around the room, his eyes settling on one object then another, like he was playing a particularly difficult version of Kim's Game and it was vital he memorised everything in the finest detail.

Finally, there was the sound of a car pulling up outside. Sandi's granny went to the door and there was some subdued conversation.

I don't know what I expected Tom's grandfather to be like; my grandparents are ancient and walk with sticks but I wasn't prepared for this tall, solid looking man. He looked barely older than my dad. He strode into the room and stood stock still. He had on a thick tweed jacket. He studied Tom, who had got up to face him.

'I told you he had the look of your Mairi around his eyes,' Sandi's granny said.

Tom's grandfather held out a large freckled hand, he didn't smile but his face wore a look of kindness. Tom, despite his height, looked dwarfed next to his grandfather as he shook his hand.

'Well Tom,' his grandfather said as he brought round his other hand and enclosed Tom's in his clasp. 'At last.'

They held each other's look for a long time then finally Tom nodded.

When his grandfather let go of Tom's hand, he turned to me. 'And will you introduce me to your friend.'

I'd been happy to keep out of the proceedings but when I stood up, Tom put his arm around my waist. 'This is Deidre.'

'She looks like a special friend.'

Tom smiled shyly at that. 'She is.'

We all sat at the table, Tom and me facing the window and Morag and Tam, as they insisted we call them, facing each other. Before long Tom was chatting away, telling all sorts of stories about his dad, and what he remembered of his mam.

I suppose the opportunity for Tom's grandfather to talk to Tom was too good to lose and when we'd finished tea they collected up the plates, cups and saucers and took them through to the kitchen.

Sandi's granny beckoned me over to sit with her beside the fire. From the kitchen we could hear water splashing into the sink. I could imagine their masculine hands handling the delicate china, carefully washing, drying and stacking the dishes. Their voices, both low and resonant, settled in to a rhythm of question and answer, becoming fluid, like water in a deep river running over stones.

Sandi's granny had her eyes shut. I leant back in to the sofa but I kept mine open. I feared to close them, even for a second.

I gazed at a large painting on the wall above the busy sideboard. It showed stalkers bringing a hind off the hillside. I've seen similar pictures ever since I can remember, some photographs, others, like this one, large oil paintings.

It was autumn in the picture, the hills purple with heather. Thick clouds, heavy with rain, were piled on top of one another. A large man strode across the hillside leading a pony; a dead hind was draped across the pony's back. A younger man followed behind. I stared at the picture and realised the figures were moving. I watched their progress down the hill, and as the older man plodded on resolutely the younger man checked the pony occasionally, examining the hind. I could tell that it was his first time stalking and he was eager to learn.

Sandi's granny stirred in her chair. I turned to watch her face as I heard her voice in my head, 'They have a good future together.'

I looked back at the picture. The figures were still again but the stance of the two men was of Tom and his grandfather.

Maybe Sandi's granny would have heard me if I'd asked the question in my head but I spoke it out loud. 'Is this how it's going to be for me?'

She nodded. Her eyes were still closed but I knew she had understood that I meant was I going to continue seeing visions? – possible glimpses into the future.

She opened her eyes and reached out to take my fingers in her own papery hands.

'You've experienced a lot of emotions recently.' Her voice was soft but audible, not a mind-voice this time. 'Jealousy, the pain of betrayal, fear ... and love. All are triggers for those who allow themselves to see and who cherish their gift.'

'A gift. Really?' I thought.

She made that strange gurgling noise in her throat. I took it for a laugh. 'I can't say how it will be for you,' she went on, 'but I too had to learn to accept and trust my visions, and enjoy them when I could.'

The conversation switched to inside my head. A question hovered that I didn't want to voice out loud. 'Is it anything to do with Tom?'

'Love is a strong force,' was what I heard.

Tom's grandfather was eager to give us a lift in his Land Rover and he dropped me off at home before taking Tom back to Mrs Fraser's.

I had a message from Frankie: 'can't do the maths, coming round' and then it was like any other Sunday evening: Frankie and me trying to get homework done before Monday morning.

Twenty-one

John's van was parked outside school when I came out on Monday afternoon. I started to walk towards the van, as I had so many times before, then I realised what I was doing. I didn't know that John was there to see me – probably not after what I presumed had taken place at Sandi's – but when I changed direction to walk home he came running towards me.

'Thought I'd give you a lift. Under the circumstances.'

'Well, okay.' I wanted to refuse but didn't want to make a fuss outside school.

'Did Sandi apologise?' he asked as I got in the van.

'What for?'

'She promised she would explain.'

'John, I'm fine with you seeing other people.' Although I wasn't sure I believed myself.

'Come on Dee. You know what Sandi's like.'

I laughed at that.

'You believe me then?' he asked.

'Yes. I believe Sandi is completely without morals and will try any trick to snare you. You'd better come in,'

I said when we reached the house. 'Mum has missed you.'

Mum was pleased to see him and gave him a big hug.

'Don't mind her,' I said, 'she's probably knocking back the cooking sherry.'

John followed me upstairs as I took my school bag to my room, like he'd done ever since we started going out. Then waited, as usual, while I went to the bathroom to change out of my school clothes. He listened to my complaining about how tedious school is and how unreasonable the teachers are and how lucky he is to be out of it and making a go of his business.

But as time crept towards five o'clock, I started anticipating Tom calling by after work. I smiled to myself as I pictured his dark wayward hair, his slightly off-centre nose and the way his serious face broke in to that heart stopping smile. My cheeks remembered the stroke of his fingertips. I tingled with remembered pleasures.

I shook myself and turned back to John. 'Look John, you don't need to keep giving me a lift. I'll be fine walking back from school.'

But John was wrapped up in his own thoughts. 'I was going to call the police but I didn't know what to tell them. I didn't see the knife. It was my fault ... again. I launched in. Matt knows how to wind me up.'

I couldn't disagree with him about that.

'Will you tell Tom I'm sorry ... and we'll sort out Matt somehow. Frankie's right. Matt can't get away with' – he threw up his hands, exasperated – 'all this.'

As John was pulling away in his van, Frankie came around the corner, walking towards the house. She looked miserable.

'What's up chick?' I asked as we shivered in the hallway.

'I've been ditched.'

'That's not possible. What happened?'

'Alec freaked when I mentioned school.'

I opened my eyes wide. 'He didn't know?'

'It's never cropped up in any of our conversations.'

'But you were having such a great time together. He's mad about you.'

'I was the mad one to fall for someone so shallow.'

'He'll be back,' I said.

'He can go boil his head. Boys ... why do we give them the time of day?' She pulled her scarf tighter around her neck and squatted on the bottom stair. 'But what I came to tell you is that Matt and Alec haven't been on speaking terms since that gig after Christmas. So, no help there.'

'Did he say why they weren't speaking?'

'They fell out that night, I think. Alec wouldn't say why.'

'Well, thanks for asking,' I said. She stood up and leaned against the front door, her face a picture of misery. 'You really did like him though, didn't you?' I said.

'Hmm,' she murmured. 'There're plenty more whelks on the shore, I suppose.'

After she left, I went back to my room and counted the minutes before I could reasonably expect Tom to arrive.

The clock ticked relentlessly towards six o'clock,

our usual tea time; I could smell the sausages cooking. Still he hadn't arrived. I thought back to when we'd said goodbye when his grandfather had dropped me off. Had we arranged for him to come by after work? I couldn't remember.

Mum called me down for tea. I ate in silence.

'Why don't you message him?' Mum said.

'Why don't you keep out of it?' I said running back up to my room.

Yet, I was so worried that he might have been attacked by Matt that I did contact him, 'are you coming over?' The message remained undelivered.

I felt stuck and stranded, and annoyed at being stuck and stranded. I felt annoyed with Tom for not coming around, annoyed with Mum for being understanding, annoyed with Frankie for being ditched and miserable, and annoyed with Sandi for trying it on with my ex-boyfriend.

I lay on my bed, thumped my pillows and cuddled up to Ted.

I was dragged from my self-pitying by the delivered tone on my phone, and then a few moments later the message received tone. It was from Tom, 'on my way.'

He looked miserable too.

'I've had to clean up some graffiti,' he said when he finally got around to admitting something was bothering him.

'Why did you have to do that?'

'It wasn't very polite,' was all he would say.

I would have questioned him further about it but he

fell on my bed, beads of sweat forming on his forehead.

'What is it?' I asked. He held his hand to his side. 'It's your wound isn't it?'

He nodded and I stroked the hair from his forehead. He was burning up.

'Come on. I'll get Mum to take you home. You'll have to let Mrs Fraser look at it.'

Mrs Fraser wasted no time in examining the wound, taking Tom's temperature and then ordering him up to bed. Next, she was on the phone to the doctor who said she'd be around within half an hour. She let me take a wet cloth up to Tom and told me to hold it against his forehead if it helped him.

But he wouldn't let me make a fuss of him; he just wanted to hold my hand.

I had to leave when the doctor arrived. Mum took me back home and I went straight to my room. I didn't even thank Mum, or apologise to her for being unreasonable earlier.

I lay flat on my bed. My arms and legs felt heavy and strangely detached, as if I had no control over them.

I stared at the ceiling. Swirls of colours passed before my eyes making strange patterns like psychedelic clouds in a child's painting. Then the swirls took on more definite shapes until I could distinguish a familiar figure in a now familiar place.

Twenty-two

Next morning, I knew what I needed to do.

I went to school as usual and spent the morning going over my plans – not that they amounted to much. At the change of each lesson I looked out the windows to watch the unrelenting torrent of rain. I sat with Frankie at lunch and when it was time to go back to class we parted; she went in to the Art room for the afternoon and I made my way towards the science labs. But I didn't join my class. I waited in a toilet for things to settle down, then I walked along the corridor holding out a piece of paper, looking purposeful. Next it was a quick dash to get out the main door.

I'd stashed my school bag in my locker – that would have to stay there until tomorrow – but I managed to pick up my jacket before escaping without being seen by the eagle-eyed secretary.

Getting there seemed to take forever. The paths were slippy with mud. My jacket was sodden before I'd left the village, and rain soaked my thin school trousers, making them stick to my legs.

I resisted going straight in. I trusted my vision that I would see him arriving. A few alder trees were growing along the crumbling edges of the swollen burn. They would provide scant protection from the deluge and no cover at all against being seen. But I couldn't stand out on the open hillside.

I hunched against one of the slim trunks and settled down to watch. I clutched my arms around my stomach to quell my shivers.

There was nothing to do now but wait.

Then he came.

He strode purposefully, leaning in to the wind, his black spider legs eating up the distance between us. He didn't see me. He wasn't looking. He was focused on the track. Then he disappeared into the low stone building.

Rain bounced in the puddles made large by the snow melt. The door to the bothy leaned open on its one hinge, causing a small patch of light to fall on the floor inside. His footprints in the mud led up to the door. I took a large breath and walked in.

Matt was facing the wall at the opposite side of the bothy. He was holding up a spray can of paint. He heard me coming in and swung around. He let out a gasp. I'd taken him by surprise. Part one of the plan accomplished. Unfortunately, there was only a part one. He looked behind me, at the doorway.

'I'm on my own,' I said.

'Why're you here?' He didn't let me answer. His face took on his customary sneer. 'He's letting you do his dirty work for him is he?'

'I don't know what you mean.'

Matt started tossing the spray can from one hand to another, making it sail higher through the air at each pass. 'He doesn't want to meet me face to face?'

'He'd be here if he could. Trouble is, he's pumped full with antibiotics to fight off an infection. He told the doctor he fell onto something sharp.'

Matt shrugged. 'Sure he's not quivering outside, too scared to come in?'

'I told you. I'm here alone,' I said. 'To see you.'

He moved towards me. 'How brave.' He puffed out his chest. 'How did you know I was here? You been following me?'

'No.' I hesitated. 'I guessed you'd want to come here.'

'You know nothing about me. You and all your goody-goody friends.' He spat on the ground next to my feet.

I felt my anger rising. 'Well ... now is your chance to tell me.'

'As if! It's none of your business,' he said.

'I think it is my business if you're going to carry on a hate campaign against Tom. He's told me about the bad history between your two families.'

'Told you his side of it you mean. And he couldn't let it rest could he. He had to come back here and stir up all the trouble again.'

'But he didn't know who you were before Christmas.'

Matt took another step towards me. He curled his top lip in malice. 'He knew my family still lived around here, knew that they would want to get even when he showed his face. He should have kept away.'

'But you can't go around causing fights. My friend got carted off to hospital because of you.'

'Always my fault isn't it. Your precious John is no better.'

I went to the fireplace and lifted the biscuit tin from the hearth.

'Hey. What do you think you're doing?' Matt said.

'I just thought I might light a fire. I don't know about you but I'm freezing.'

He didn't say anything to stop me, so I crouched down, opened the biscuit tin and took out matches, a few curls of wood shavings and some dry sticks. I looked at my hands, I felt sure they would be shaking but I was pleased to see they were rock solid. I placed the thin shavings and the tiny sticks in the grate and struck a match. It flared on the first strike. The few orange flames licking around the fuel were small comfort in the gloomy room but I felt a renewed courage. Some fir cones that Tom and I had collected lay scattered on the hearth. Most were tightly closed with the damp air but a couple were slightly open; I put those close to the flames.

Matt moved towards the fire and stared into it. He looked mesmerised.

I thought I'd try a change of subject. 'How's Stephie?' I asked.

'What's it to you?'

'She seems nice.'

'Lots of people think so.' He made it sound like a

crime to be popular and I said as much.

'She's not a patch on Amy,' he said.

'You like Amy then?'

'Surprised, are you? You don't think much of her, do you?'

'I'm not surprised that you should like Amy. She's very ... attractive.'

'She's more than that.'

'But you called her a slut!'

'I was only winding John up. Amy knows I didn't mean it.'

'And you were trying to chat up Frankie.'

'Ha. I had a bet with Alec that I could cop off with her first. Then I saw Amy at the dance. She was up for a good time.'

I was thinking about what Frankie had said about Matt and Alec falling out so I wasn't ready for what happened next.

I don't know what spooked him but suddenly Matt launched towards me, grabbed my wrist and pulled my arm up behind my back.

'You're hurting me,' I yelled.

'That's what I do isn't it? Hurt people.'

He knocked me on the floor then went back to the fireplace and kicked out the small fire that was growing in the grate. He turned to face me. 'So. Go on. What are you doing here?'

I pulled myself up to standing. 'I told you, I came to talk to you. Tom's sick. No-one knows I'm here.' I was hit by the truth of it.

He must have believed me because he calmed down a bit. He came towards me and leaned over, his breath coming out in quick spurts. 'So, you thought you'd follow me?' he said, his face too close to mine.

I continued with the truth. 'I didn't ... follow you. I knew you'd come here. I ... saw us talking in here. I thought I could help.'

'What do you mean 'saw us'?'

'I see ... things.'

'What do you mean?' he asked again. 'Like in seeing the future.'

'Kind of.'

'Did you see this?' He took hold of a handful of my hair and pulled it down, hard enough to hurt.

I kept my head upright, straining against the pull of my hair. 'No,' I said looking him in the eyes. 'Tom understands why you're angry. He knows about your family. But, surely, it's so long ago,' I said.

'Not so long ago for my grandfather. Can you imagine what he's had to put up with? No one has ever cleared his name.' He let go of my hair but his face was still just a few centimetres from mine. I could see the blood vessels throbbing on his temple.

He picked up the spray can again and going back to the wall he started spraying; the black paint spluttered out forming crude letters that spelled 'gypsy rapist'.

'That's what my grandfather has lived with all his life,' he said.

'I know how to get his name cleared,' I said.

Matt snorted. 'Little Miss Fix-it, aren't you?'

He came towards me again, still holding the paint can. He pointed it at my face. Instinctively, I closed my eyes. I heard the hiss of the paint sputtering out but I felt nothing; he'd sprayed the wall at my side.

He seemed to be thinking what to do next. Maybe he would have listened to me but a shadow blocked the small amount of light coming through the door. I looked towards it and Matt swivelled around. Frankie burst in through the doorway.

'Bitch!' Matt spat at me. He flew across to the door but another figure came in: the huge bulk of Tom's grandfather. Matt squirmed as Big Tam grabbed him by the arm like he was a dishrag.

'Glad to make your acquaintance,' Big Tam said to Matt. 'I believe I owe your grandfather – and you – an explanation and an apology.'

Matt looked completely deflated, but he kept throwing me and Frankie evil looks as we all trooped out of the bothy and along the croft track. Big Tam had brought his Land Rover as far as he could, and when we reached it Frankie and I climbed in the back while Matt slid in the front passenger seat.

We were back in the village in no time and Big Tam dropped me and Frankie at mine before going on to town with Matt.

'Don't you ever do anything like that ever again. That boy is a psycho. Who knows what would have happened to you if me and Big Tam hadn't got to you when we did.' Frankie was fuming when she'd bundled me up to my bedroom. Then she relented.

'Did he hurt you at all?' she asked, holding me by my shoulders and questioning me deeply with her eyes.

'No. He scared me quite a bit but he didn't hurt me.'

Frankie quickly filled me in with her part of the story – telling me about how she'd missed me at the end of school and knew something was wrong; about how she'd seen Big Tam heading up to the bothy in his Land Rover. He'd stopped and asked her to go with him and on the way, he'd talked about Sandi's granny having 'seen' something going on there.

'Why didn't you tell me? What made you go off on your own?' she said.

'You wouldn't have let me go.'

'Too right I wouldn't.'

'And I saw just me and Matt talking.'

'Another vision?' she asked.

I nodded.

'This is really happening to you isn't it?'

I nodded again.

'How are you coping with it?'

'Not very well,' I managed to say through a tight throat.

'Tell me all about it.'

She listened patiently. She stroked my hair. She made sympathetic noises. And – she had to admit that I was experiencing unusual insights.

'Maybe you are psychic or something,' she said.

'But why me? I've never so much as had bad dreams before. Nothing unusual ever happens to me.'

'I can't answer that one,' she said. 'But hey, maybe we won't have to read the horoscopes anymore.' I knew she was trying to make light of it to make me feel better.

'There's one good thing though,' she said.

'And that is?'

'You can use your phone without worrying. You can delete as many names as you like. Go on, try deleting my name.'

I thought she was only joking but she went on. 'Go on. You know your phone isn't causing bad things to happen. Delete my name to prove it.' And she fixed me with her look while I took out my phone and deleted her name from the contacts list. I didn't see any pictures in my head, or images on the ceiling; there were no bangs or flashes in my brain. Then she took out her battered phone and sent me a message. 'love you' it read.

'You can save my number again now,' she said.

'Remind me to get Dad to send you a new phone for your birthday.'

'I think I'll pass on that,' she said.

Twenty-three

'Not another party,' Tom said checking his phone. We were putting together our lunch in Mrs Fraser's kitchen. 'Don't you lot ever stop?'

'Just wait until February. Nothing happens then.' I realised what I'd said. Tom wouldn't be here in February to see us, whether we were hectic or not.

My phone received a message too, 'Old New Year ceilidh. Be there. Sandi xx'

'Do you want to go?' I asked. The doctor had signed Tom off work for a week and he'd spent the first few days in bed, his temperature fluctuating wildly. He'd had plenty of visitors though, including daily calls from Big Tam. Mrs Fraser had promised that if he stayed in during the week, she would let him out at the weekend but I didn't want to take things too far.

'I don't think Sandi will let us miss it, will she?' Tom said.

'Let's see how you feel after we've been up to the bothy.'

It was Baltic in the bothy. We got a fire going straight away but we could still see our breath although the flames were leaping up the chimney. Tom's homemade cushions and the hessian curtains were dank and musty smelling.

'Not very homely,' Tom said, and I agreed.

We decided to have a scout about outside for more pinecones while the fire warmed the large room. We brought back fresh heather and even though it was damp it was still springy. We covered it with blankets. Eventually, we warmed up in the nest we made for ourselves. The large candles were still in place and they burned with a steady flame, making soft shadows dance on the low ceiling. I'd brought a flask of hot chocolate so we didn't need to wait for a kettle to boil. As we unpacked the food, Tom brought out a separate parcel wrapped in greaseproof paper. He tossed it to me.

'What is it?'

'Open it and see.'

It was the wrong shape for sandwiches or cake. I prodded it.

'Open it,' he said again.

I pulled the crinkled paper apart and gasped. In the parcel was a wrist band worked in soft, deep-red leather. An intricate Celtic knot pattern twisting in a continuous spiral was delicately carved in the surface. Tom held it around my wrist and knotted the leather lace to fasten it.

'It's beautiful. Thanks.' I whispered.

'I've had a bit of spare time recently. I had to keep busy somehow.'

'You made it for me?'

'Well I tried giving it to Mrs Fraser but the colour didn't suit her.'

I hugged him tight.

'I'll have something to remember you by,' I said, trying to keep my voice even. 'And I've not given you anything. I'll have to find something to...' I felt the itch of tears that I couldn't blink away.

'Deidre—' he started.

'No ... It's okay. I know we've got to part soon. I'll live with it. You've got so much to look forward to. Do you know what you're going to do yet, by the way? Will you still keep in touch with Big Tam?' I was rambling on but if I stopped talking, I knew I would have to face up to the inevitable truth of Tom leaving. 'You'll soon forget me when you get to Canada.'

'Stop please.' Tom covered his face with his hands. 'You are about as far from the truth as you could possibly get.' He took a deep breath. 'Deidre. I've decided. I'm going nowhere.'

I stared into the fire. 'You want...' I found the courage to say it out loud, 'You want to stay?'

He turned his face towards me. 'I do,' he said. His face was serious. His jaw set firm.

'But what will you do?'

'I'll find work somewhere.'

'Can you get a job on the hydro scheme?' My mind was in turmoil. Could Tom stay around here?

'No. The jobs there will finish soon. But I can look for something else.'

'You really want to do this? Give up your course,

give up your chance to go to Canada, put up with the prejudiced idiots here?'

'I can find another course. I'll probably be able to transfer to another college if I want. As for Canada, chances are Dad will get fed up in a few months and then he'll want to be back. And, trust me, I meet prejudiced idiots wherever I stay. So, it's not all about what I'll be giving up.'

It sounded great but something niggled. I pushed my fingers through his hair. 'But what if it doesn't work out between us? How can we know?'

'We can't know if we don't try. One day at a time, right? And I want to try if you do.'

They say actions speak louder than words, don't they? I rummaged around in Tom's jacket pocket and felt for the square foil packet. It was still there.

The remains of the bonfire to celebrate the Old New Year were still burning bright in the damp air as we reached Sandi's house. Flickering sparks spat in to the night.

'Stop it,' I said as we went in the front door.

'Stop what?'

'You're grinning like a loon.'

Tom's face dropped and a frown creased his brow. 'Am I?' He grinned again. 'So I am.' We held hands; our fingers interlaced as though nothing could ever prise them apart.

Sandi was officiating in the living room where a complicated game of Twister was taking place. Several people had shoes on their hands and others seemed to have swapped clothes. John had on Sandi's halter neck top while Sandi was wearing John's denim shirt.

'Get yourselves a drink and join in,' Sandi called to us over the dance music.

Frankie was sitting on the sofa but she jumped up and hugged us both then came with us into the kitchen. The oldies were all sitting around the oak kitchen table where cans and bottles jostled for space with piles of baked potatoes and bowls of fillings. Sandi's mum and granny were there along with my mum, Mrs Fraser and Big Tam. Other assorted oldies from the village who will descend on a party at the slightest whisper were also squeezed in.

Sandi's granny was snuggled next to the Aga but she looked at bit lost without her usual cushions and rugs.

Big Tam passed us some cans of coke – Mrs Fraser making it quite clear Tom was not allowed any alcohol yet – and made room for us at the table.

'We'll have a wee ceilidh later,' Sandi's mum said. 'Frankie's brought her fiddle, haven't you dear, and Big Tam will give us a few songs. What can you do, Tom?' I had a secret thought of what Tom could do very well but I stopped myself as I glanced at Sandi's granny.

'He's going to start the line dance with me, aren't you, Tom?' Mum said.

Tom was still grinning, which I'm sure Mum took as agreement.

I looked at her wine glass. 'What number is that?'

'It's only my second. Don't be cheeky.'

The door to the kitchen burst open and Amy and

Matt came charging in.

'I don't know what I need more, a drink or a piss,' Amy was saying. They obviously hadn't been told the oldies were in here. Everyone in the kitchen fell silent. Amy was the first to recover. 'Fix me a drink, Matt, I need to go upstairs.'

Matt didn't move but Big Tam said, 'Matt.' And Matt nodded at him.

'Are you driving tonight?' Big Tam asked.

'No. We walked up from Amy's. Her mum's letting me stay there tonight.'

With that, Big Tam passed him a can of beer and Matt took a can of cider for Amy.

Then Matt turned to Frankie. 'I told Alec he'd made a big mistake letting you go. You might be stuck up but you're the best thing that's ever happened to him.' And with that he left the kitchen.

'Well, there's one thing you can give Matt credit for,' said Sandi's mum, 'he certainly doesn't hide his opinions.'

I didn't think I would ever witness what happened next: Frankie's face went a bright crimson as she blushed.

And then, as if on cue, Frankie's phone wailed out its ridiculous tone. Frankie stared at the message; her brows pulled together like she was quizzing her phone.

'Alec?' I asked.

She nodded. 'What should I do?' she whispered to me.

Tom's warmth surrounded me. 'Answer him,' I said.

I don't think Tom was aware of anything that was going on around him. He just perched next to me like a faithful spaniel. When he leaned towards me and kissed my cheek it was my turn to blush.

I pulled Tom to his feet – our hands were still firmly clasped – and led him out the back door. I didn't feel like sharing him with the rest of the crowd just yet. There would be plenty of time to join in with the party games. And Sandi deserved a chance to share more clothing with John if that was what she wanted.

Standing side by side we stared into the crackling bonfire.

'What can you see, Deidre? What does the future look like?' Tom asked.

I turned from the fire to face him and said, 'It looks good to me.'